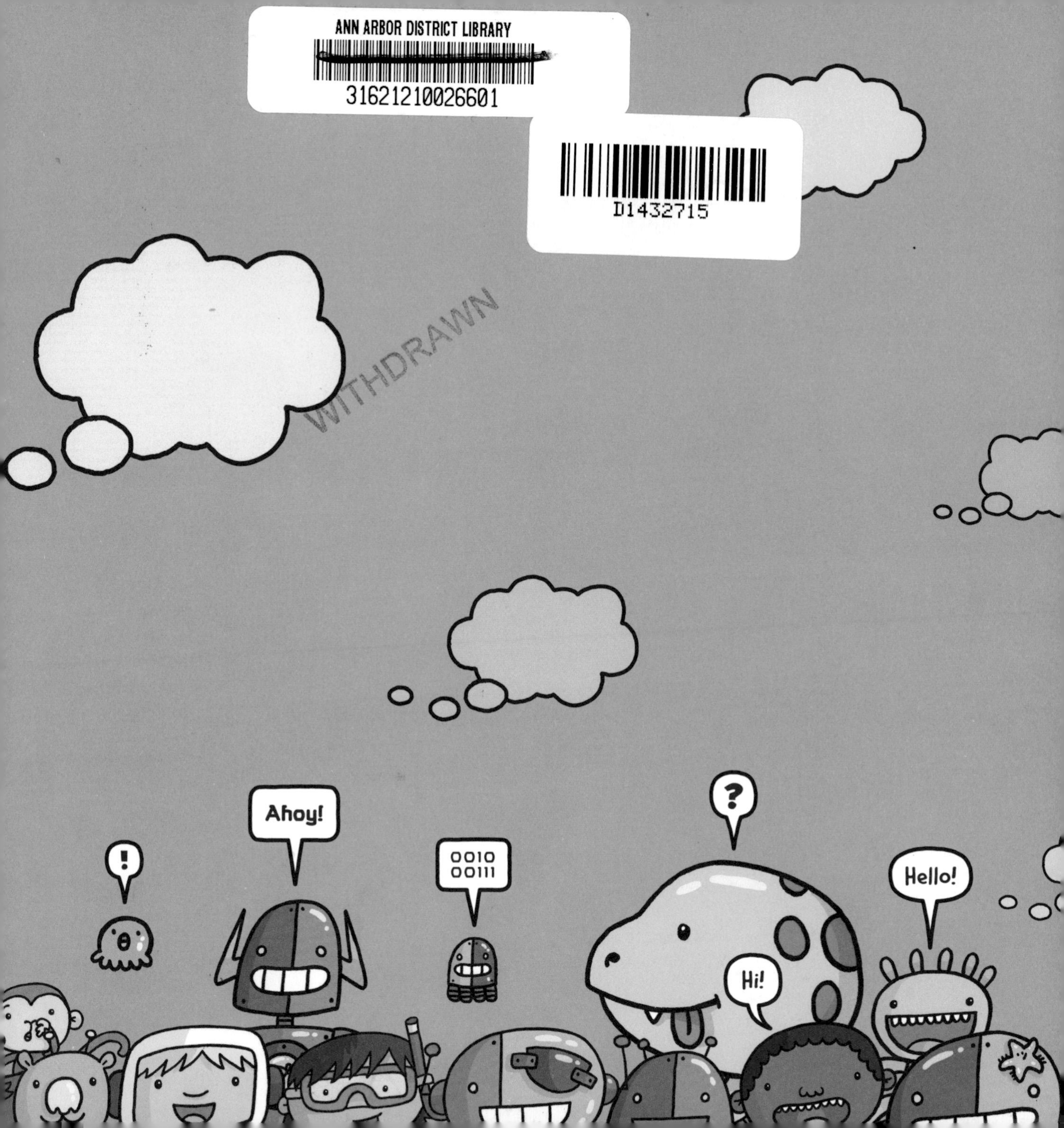
!
Ahoy!
0010
00111
?
Hi!
Hello!

COMICS LAND

by
CAPSTONE

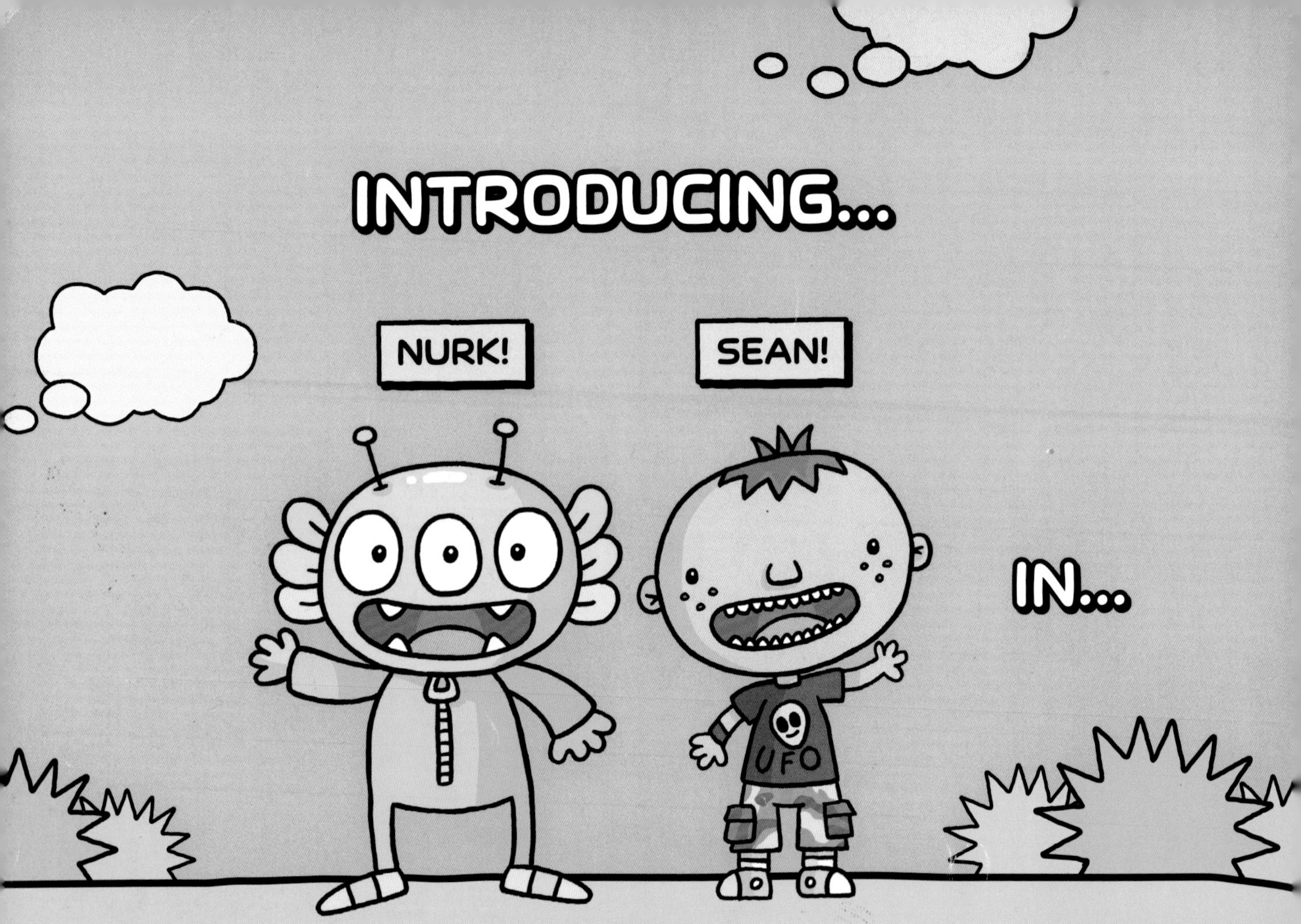
INTRODUCING...
NURK!
SEAN!
UFO
IN...

capstone
www.capstoneyoungreaders.com

1710 Roe Crest Drive, North Mankato, Minnesota 56003

Cataloging-in-Publication data is available on the Library of Congress website.
ISBN: 978-1-4342-4272-3 (hardcover) • ISBN: 978-1-4342-4032-3 (library binding)

Printed in United States of America in Brainerd, Minnesota. 092012 006938BANGS13

THE NEW KID FROM PLANET GLORF

written by
ARIE KAPLAN

illustrated by
JESS BRADLEY

designed by
BOB LENTZ

edited by
JULIE GASSMAN

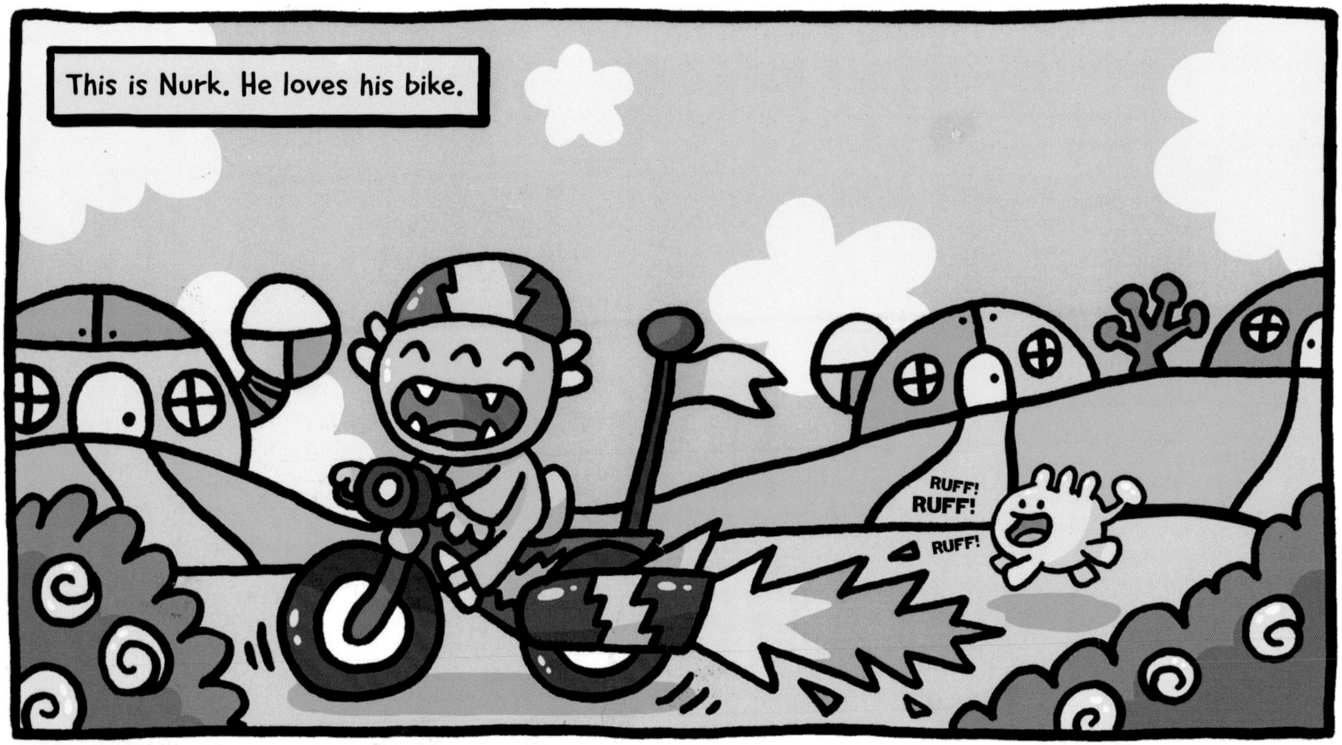
This is Nurk. He loves his bike.
RUFF!
RUFF!
RUFF!

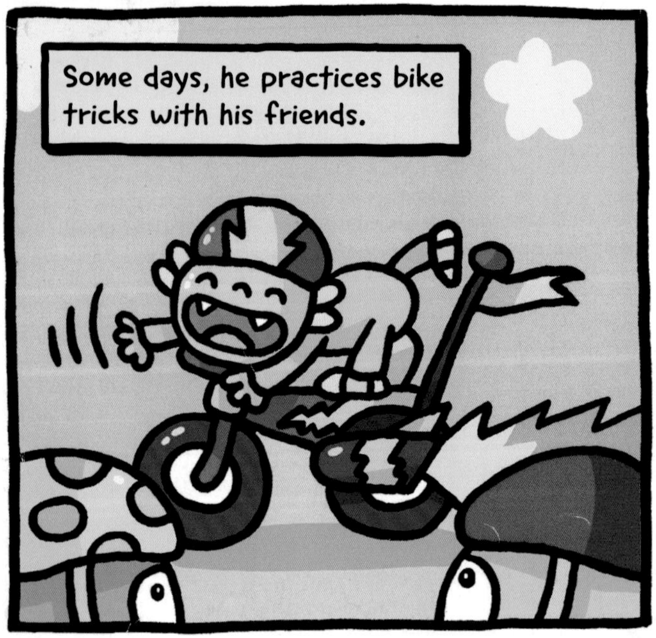
Some days, he practices bike tricks with his friends.

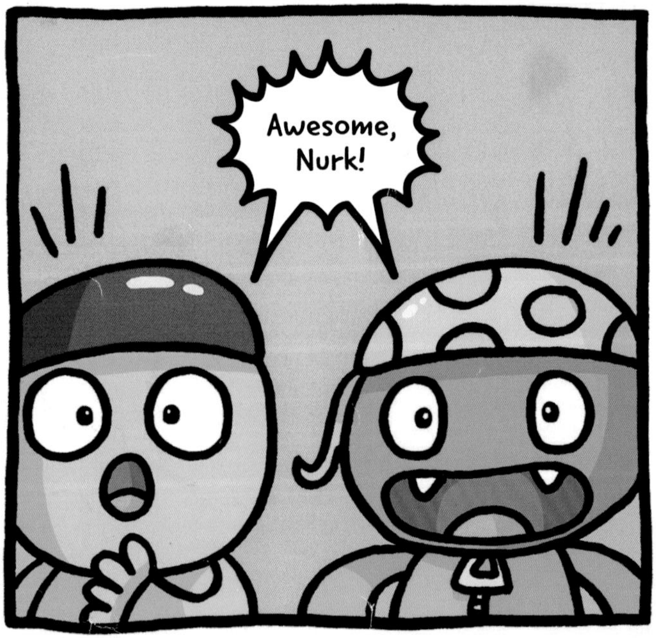
Awesome, Nurk!

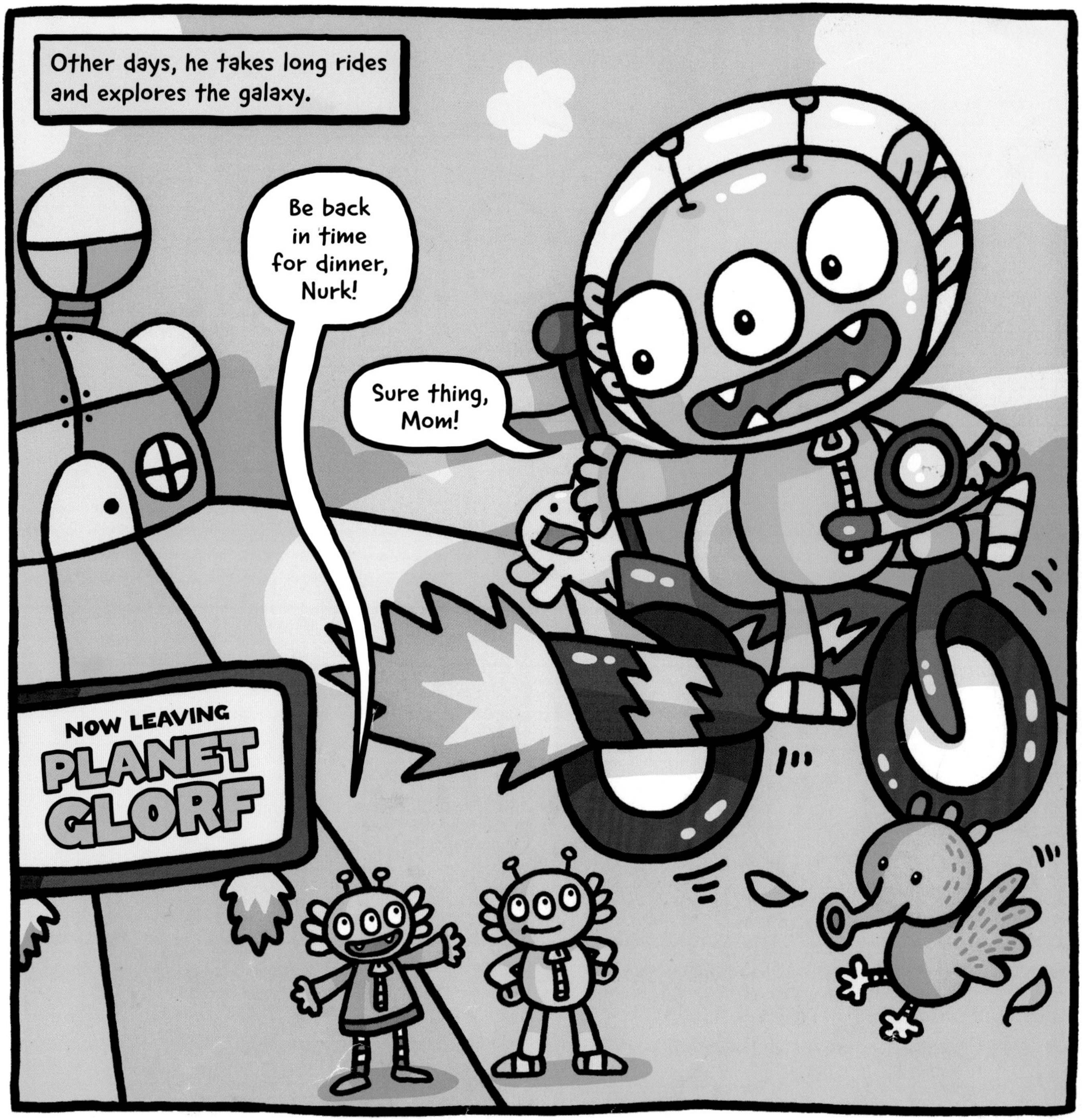

Other days, he takes long rides and explores the galaxy.
Be back in time for dinner, Nurk!
Sure thing, Mom!
NOW LEAVING PLANET GLORF

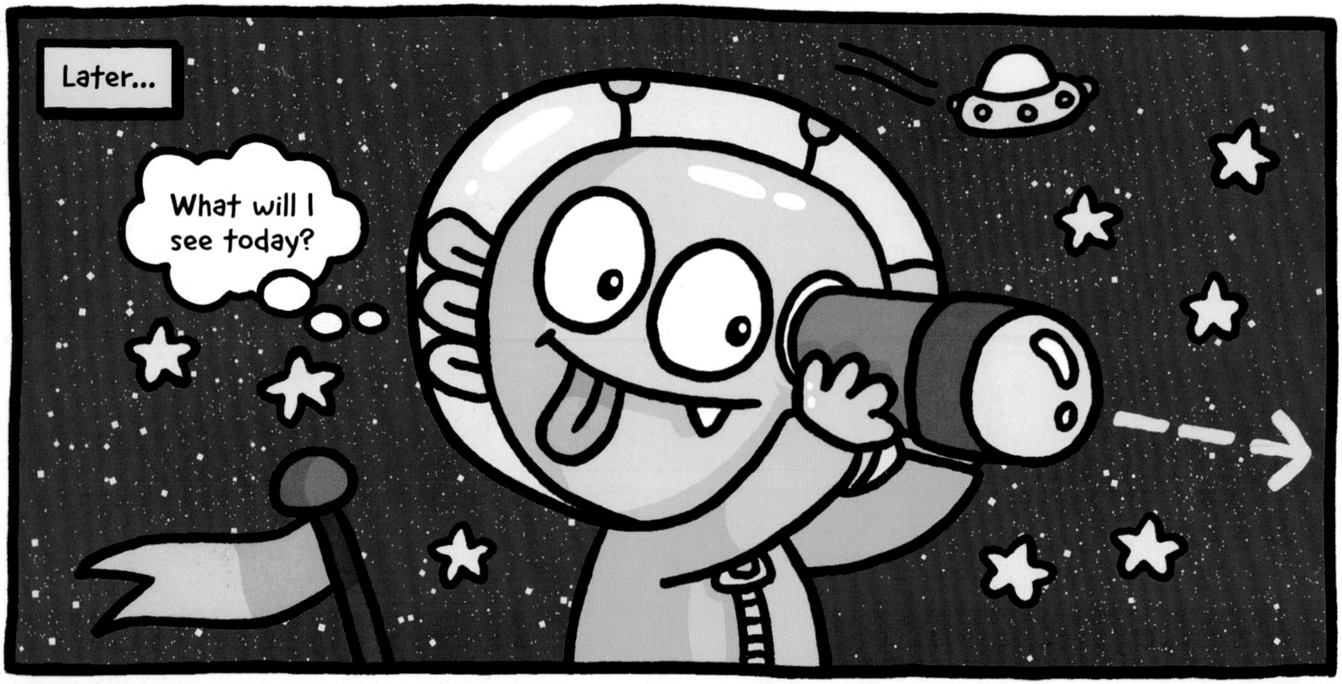
Later...
What will I see today?

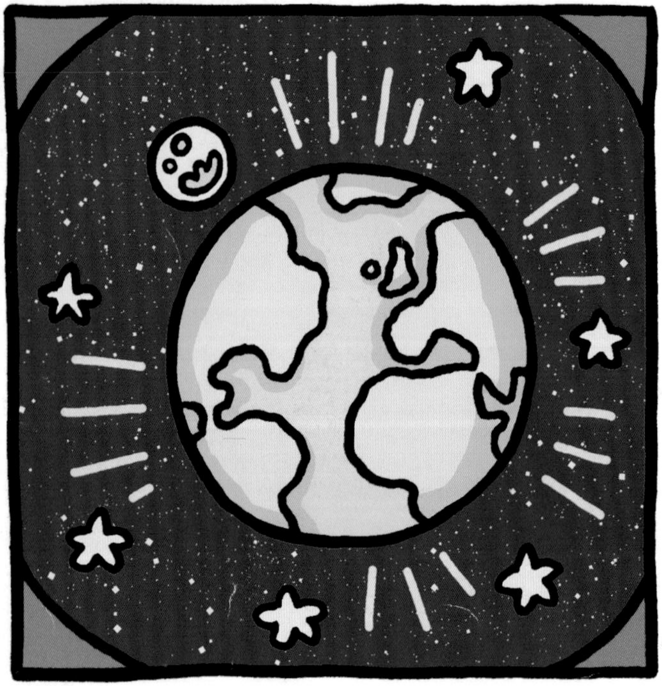

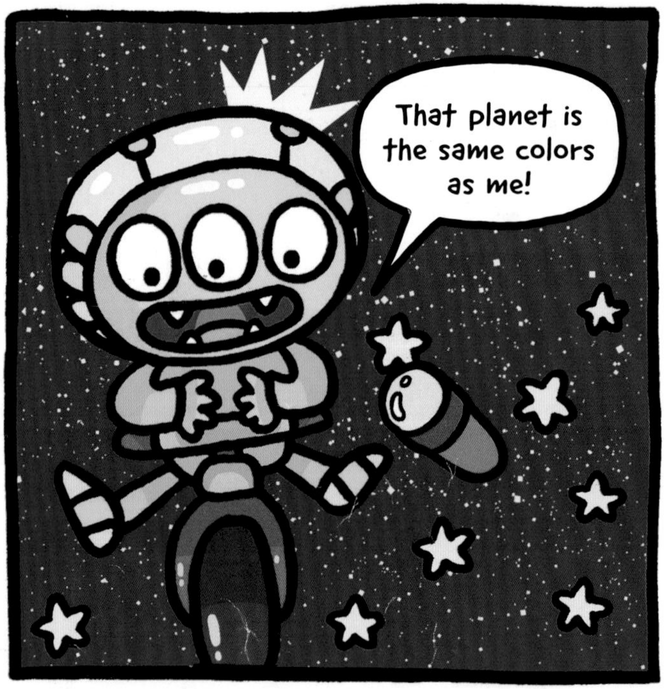
That planet is the same colors as me!

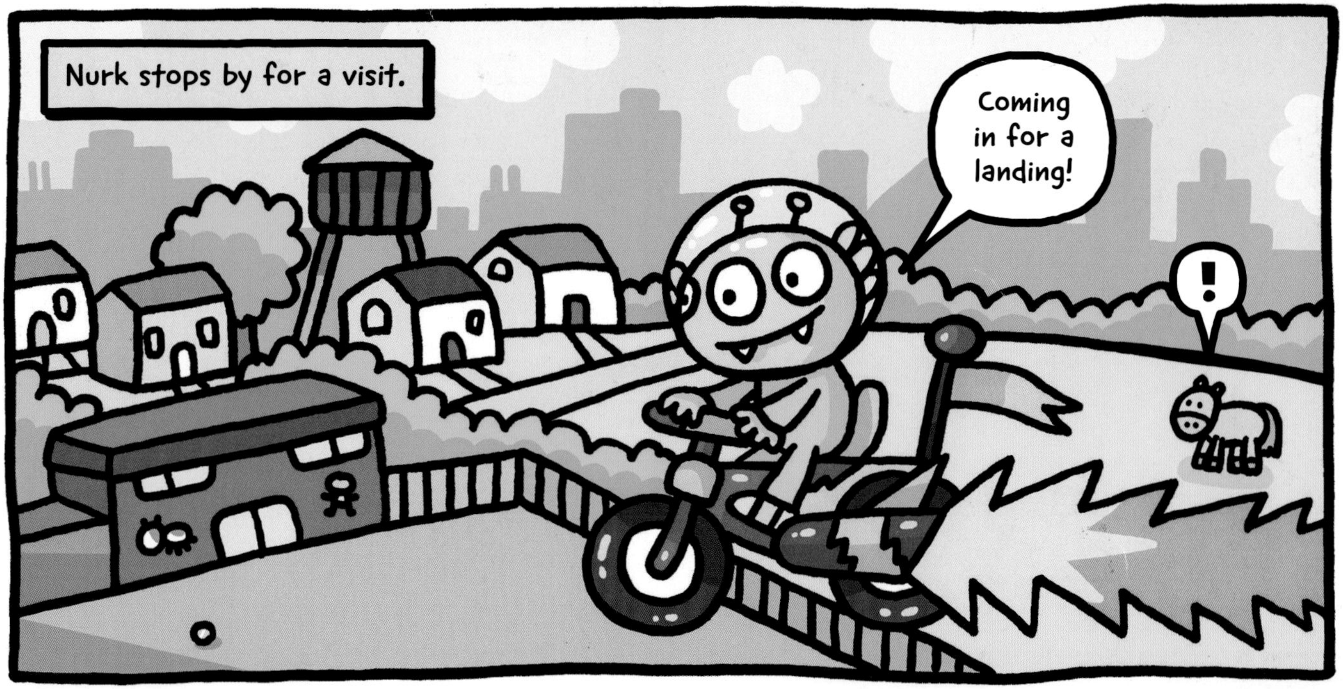
Nurk stops by for a visit.
Coming in for a landing!
!

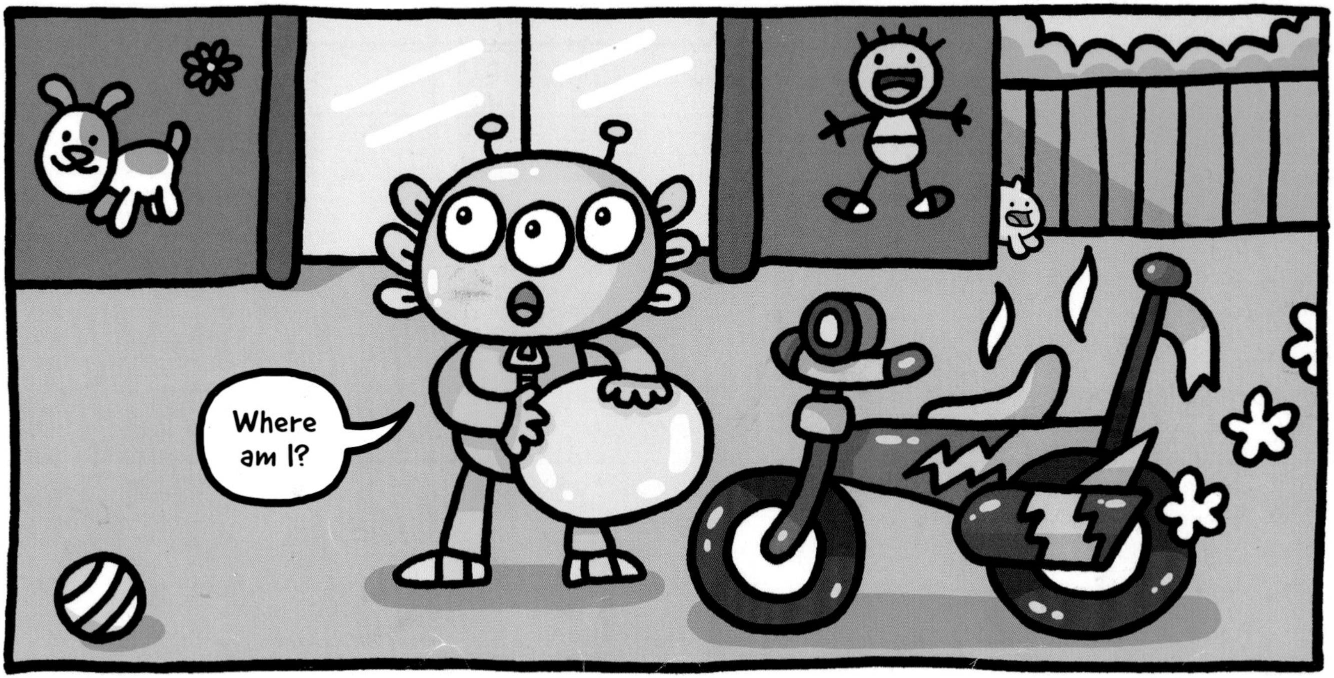
Where am I?

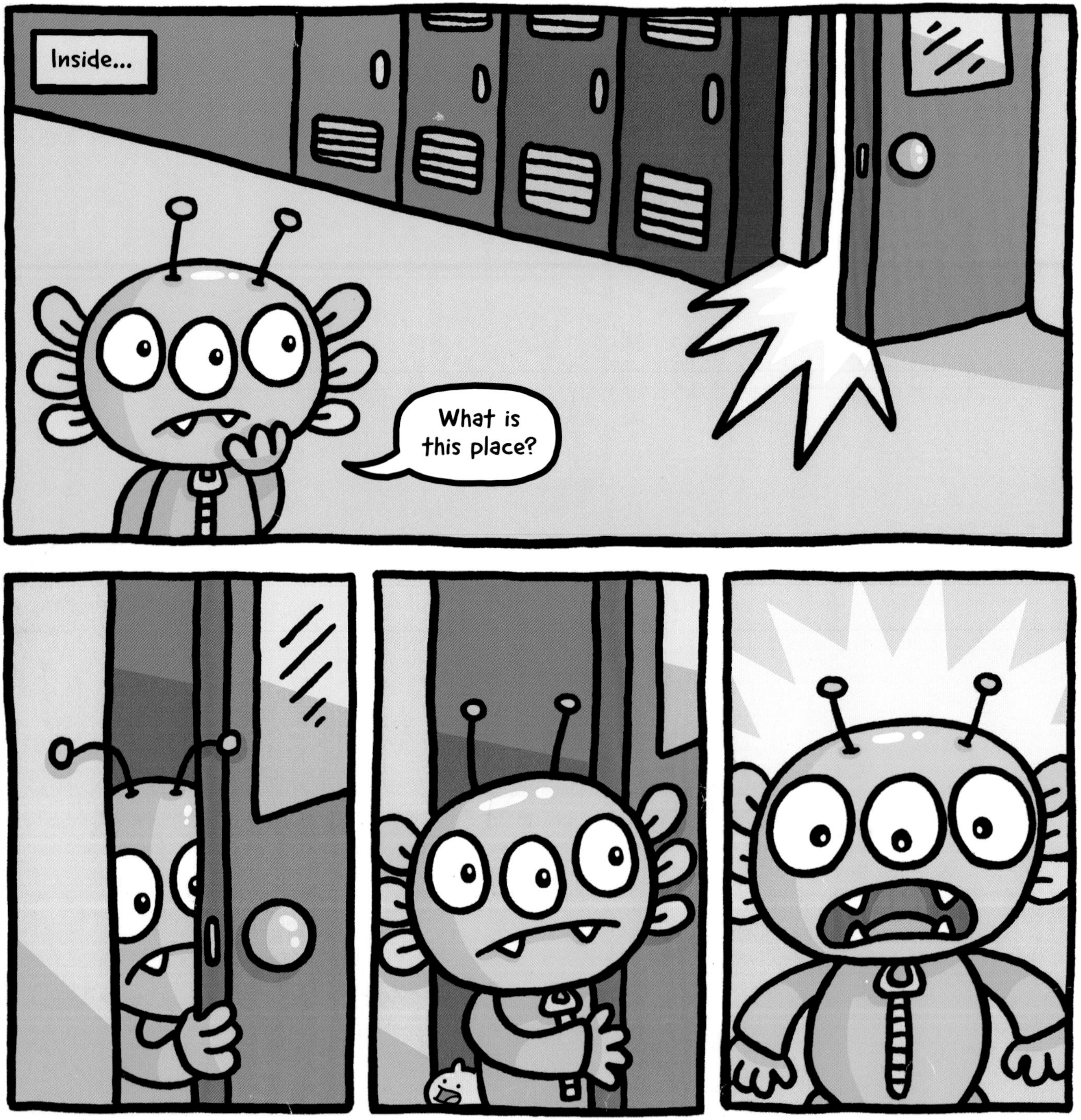
Inside...
What is this place?

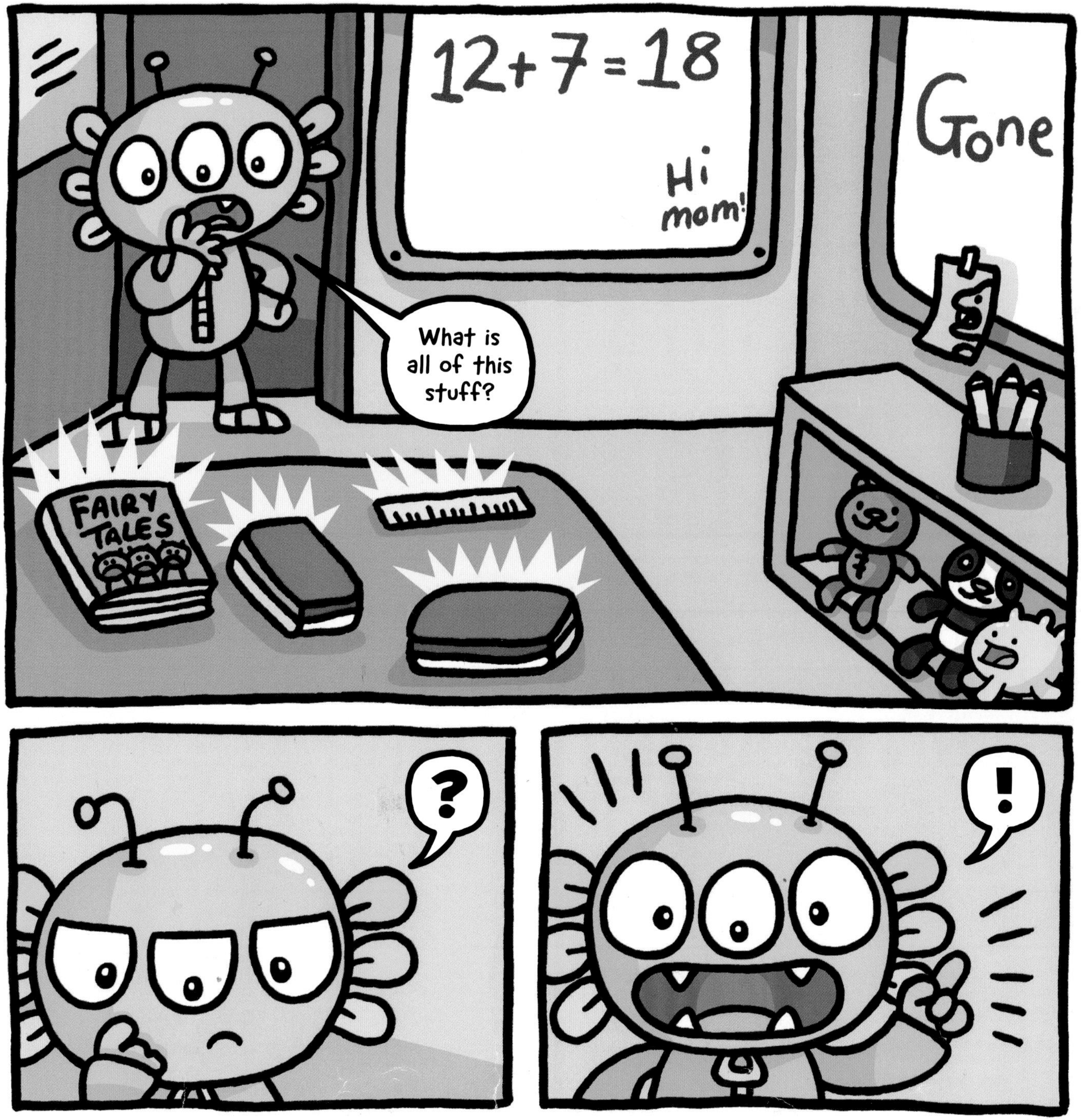
12+7=18
Hi mom!
Gone
FAIRY TALES
What is all of this stuff?
?
!

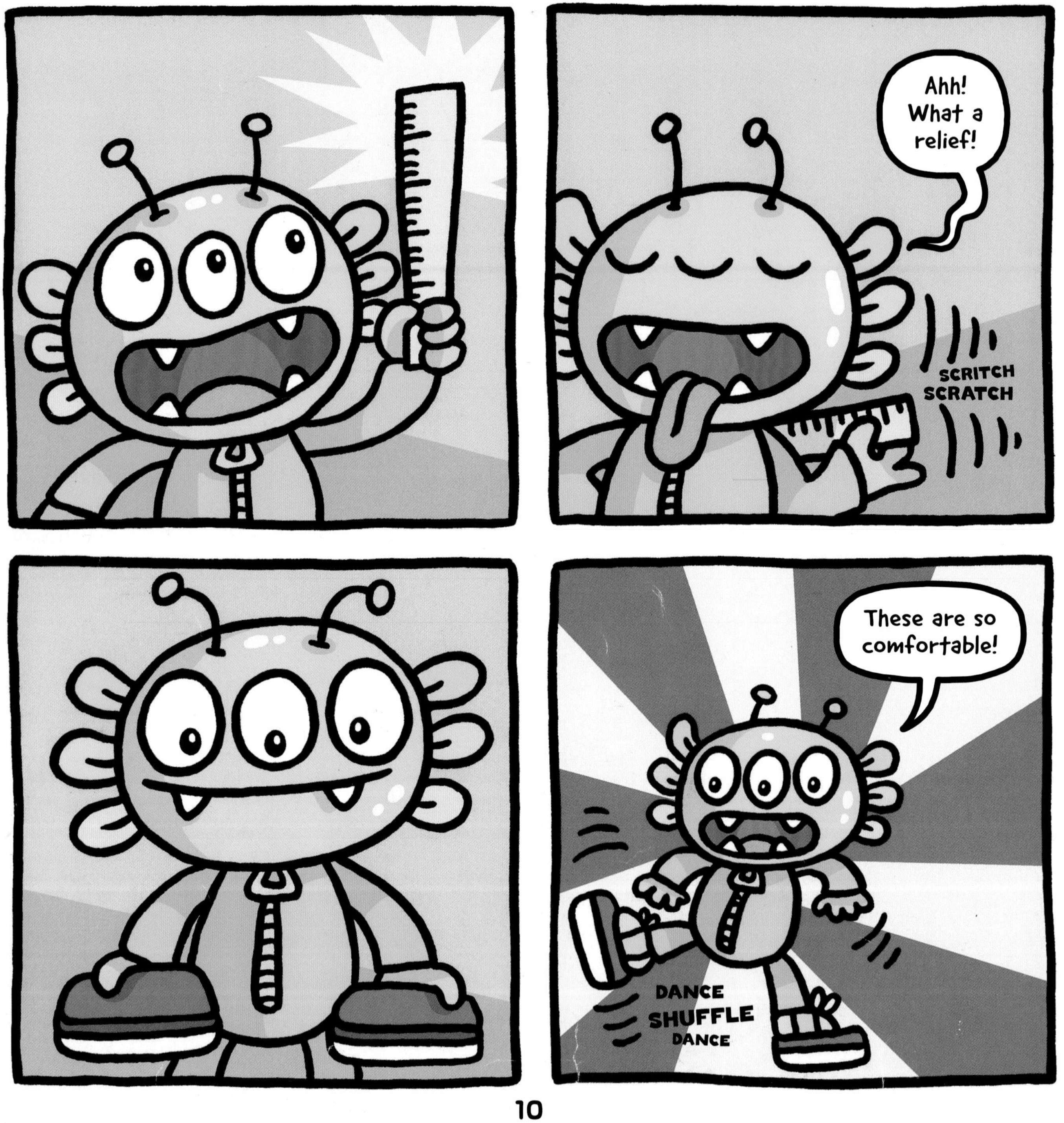
Ahh! What a relief!
SCRITCH SCRATCH
These are so comfortable!
DANCE SHUFFLE DANCE

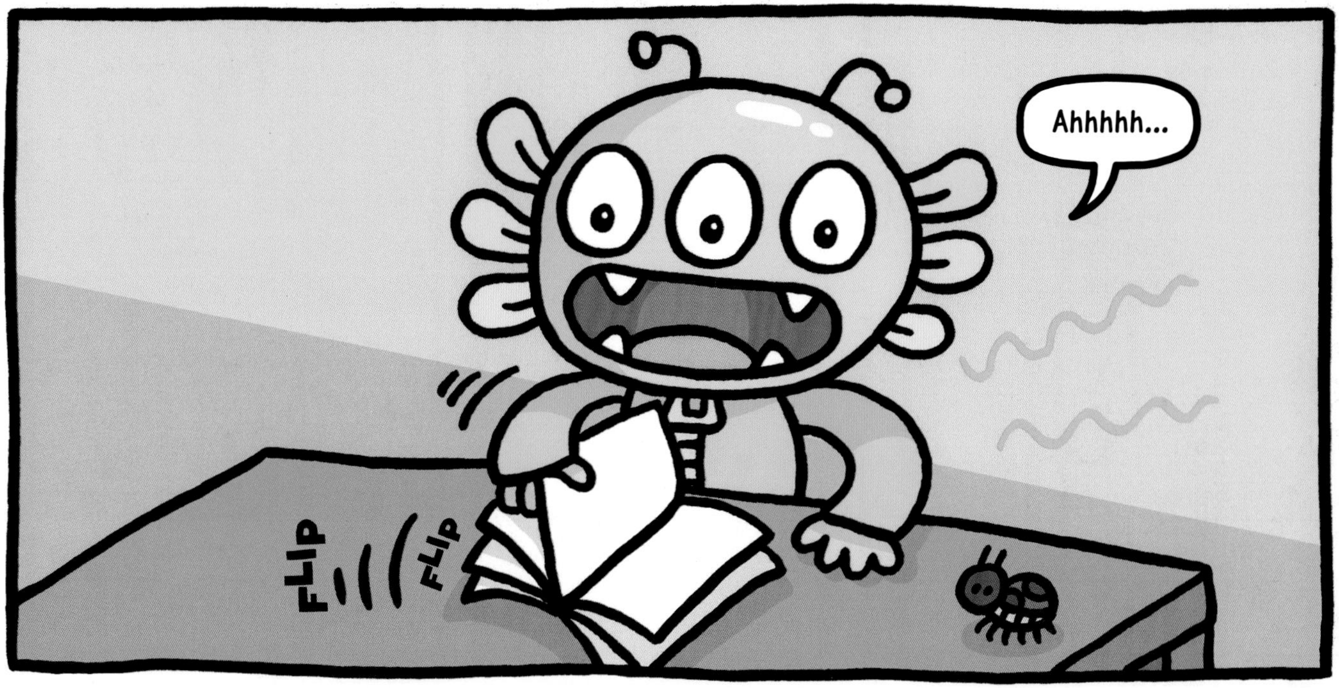
Ahhhhh...
FLIP
FLIP

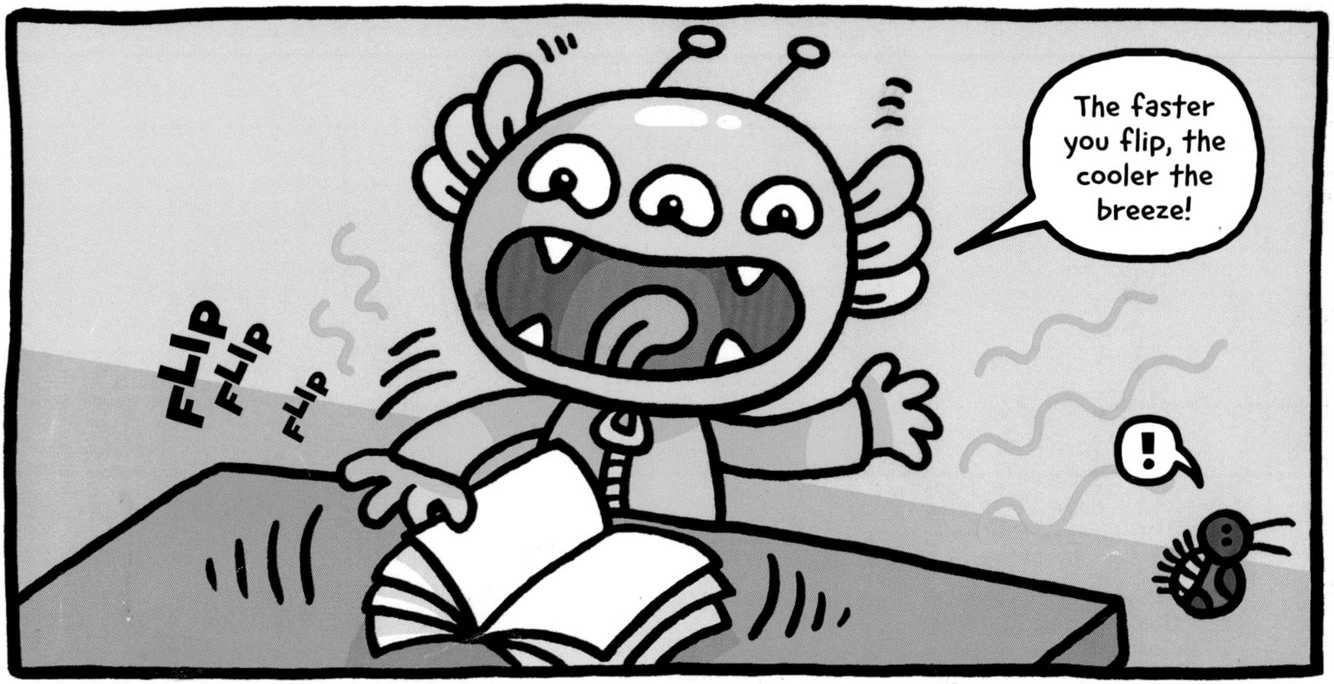
The faster you flip, the cooler the breeze!
FLIP
FLIP
FLIP
!

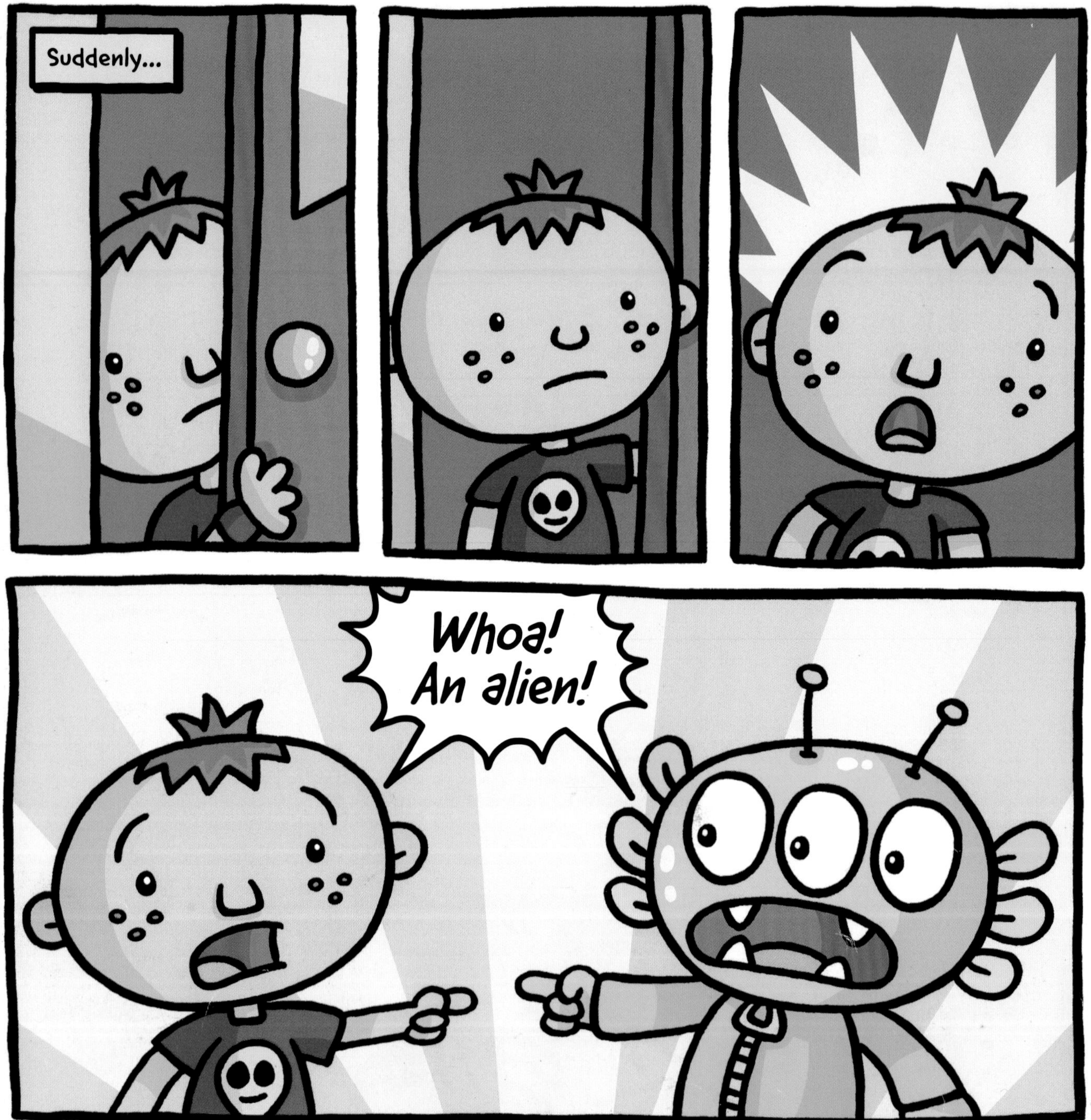

Suddenly...
Whoa! An alien!

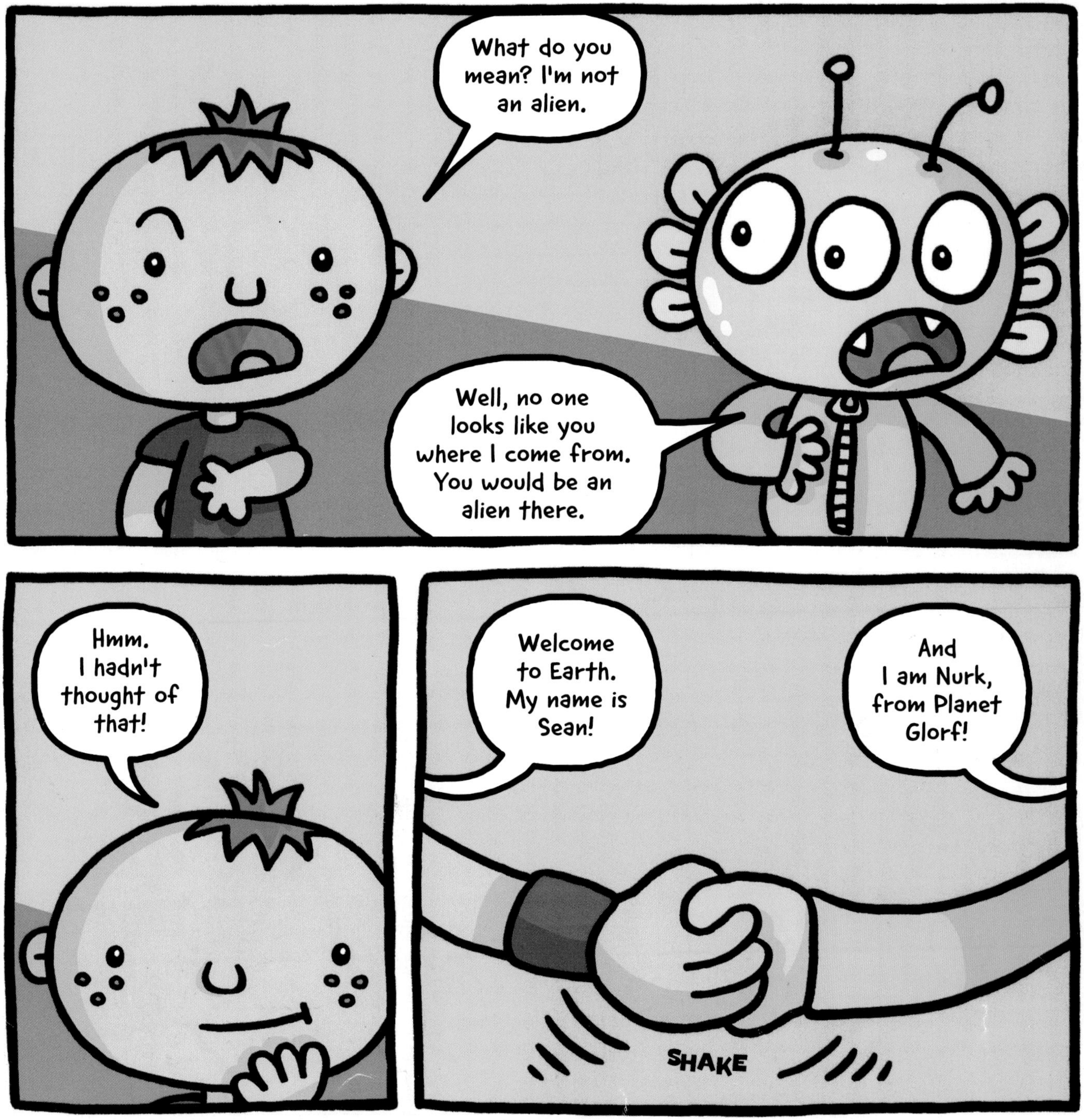
What do you mean? I'm not an alien.
Well, no one looks like you where I come from. You would be an alien there.
Hmm. I hadn't thought of that!
Welcome to Earth. My name is Sean!
And I am Nurk, from Planet Glorf!
SHAKE

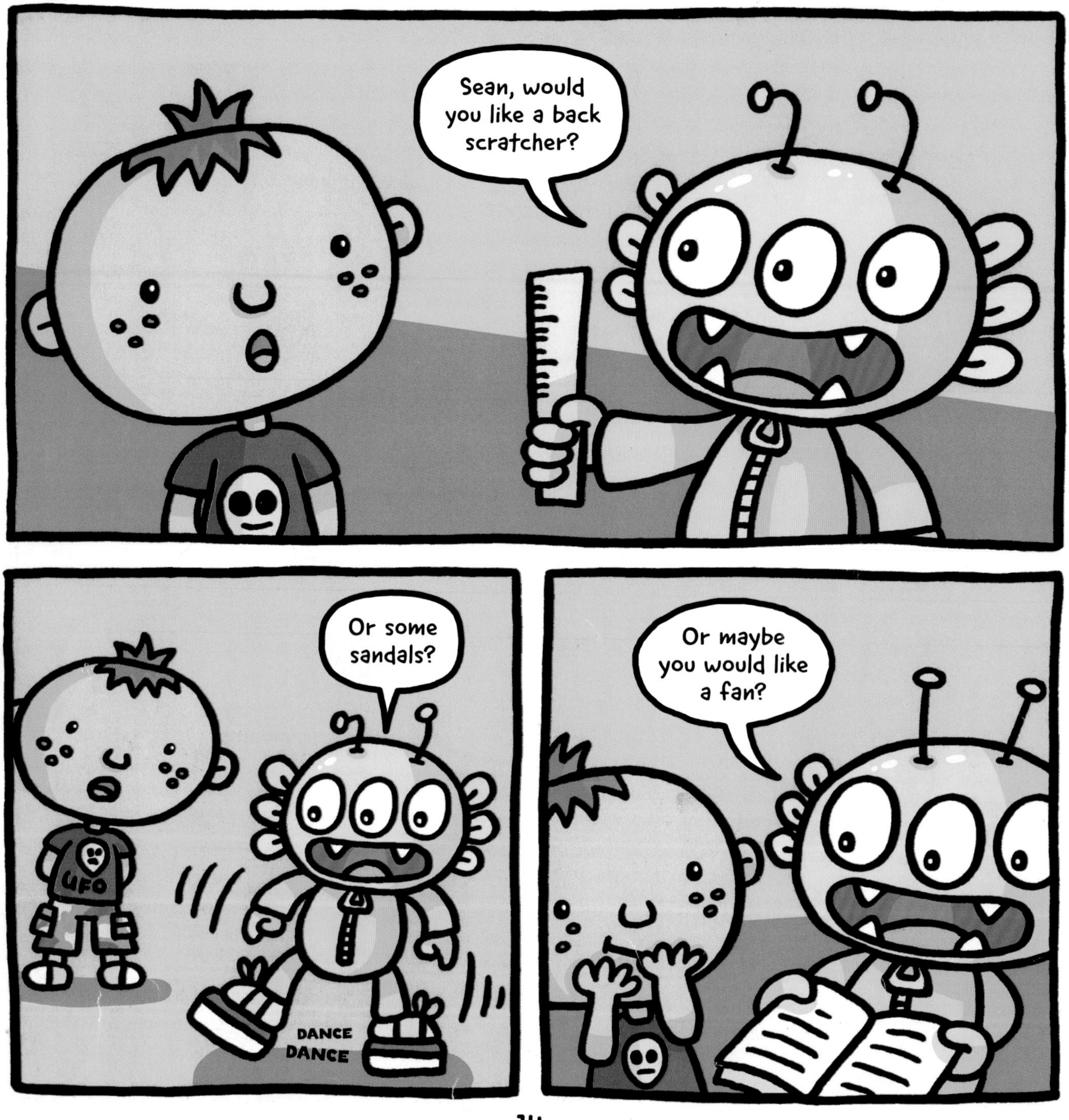

Sean, would you like a back scratcher?
Or some sandals?
UFO
DANCE
DANCE
Or maybe you would like a fan?

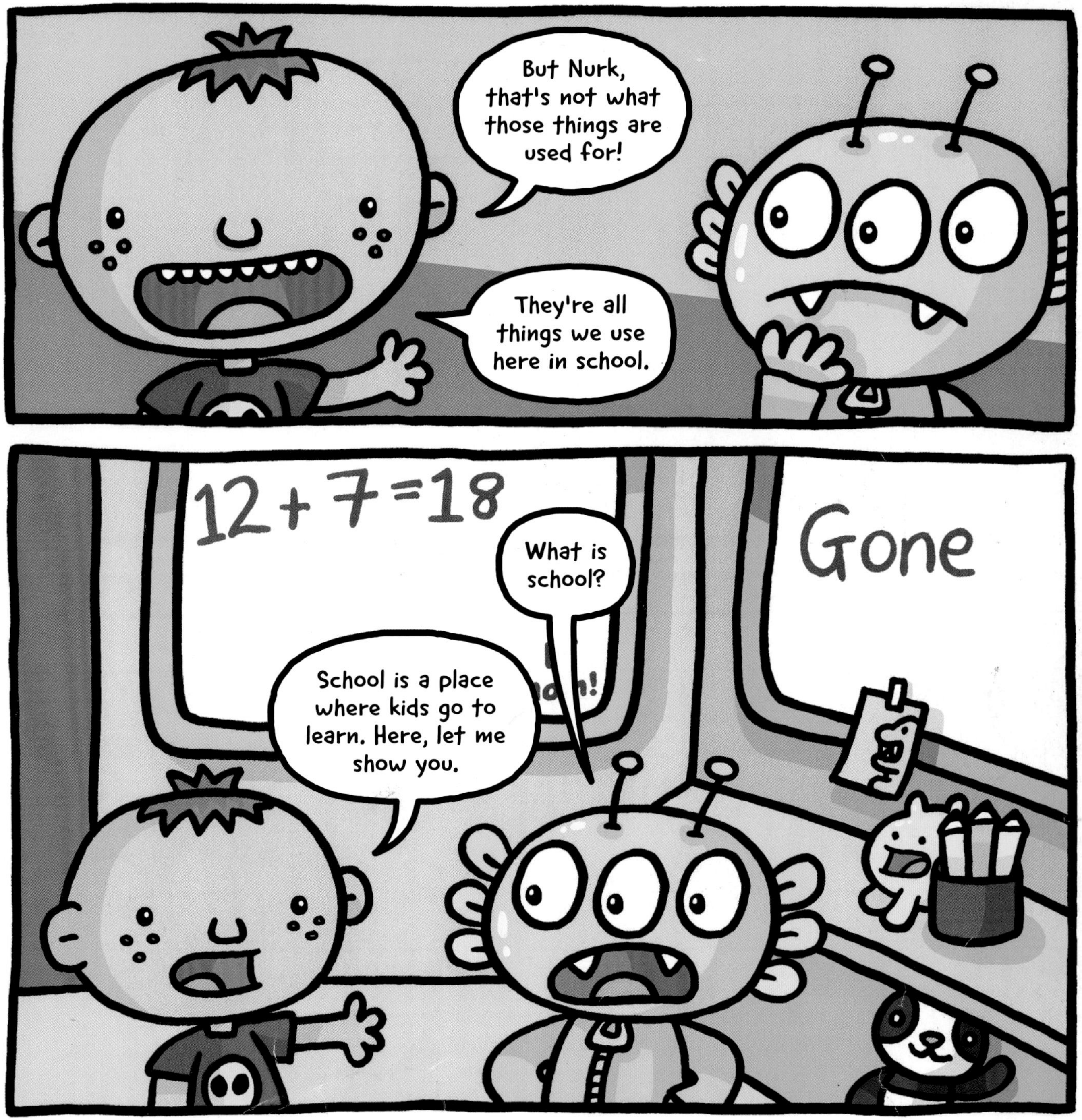

But Nurk, that's not what those things are used for!
They're all things we use here in school.
12 + 7 = 18
Gone
What is school?
School is a place where kids go to learn. Here, let me show you.

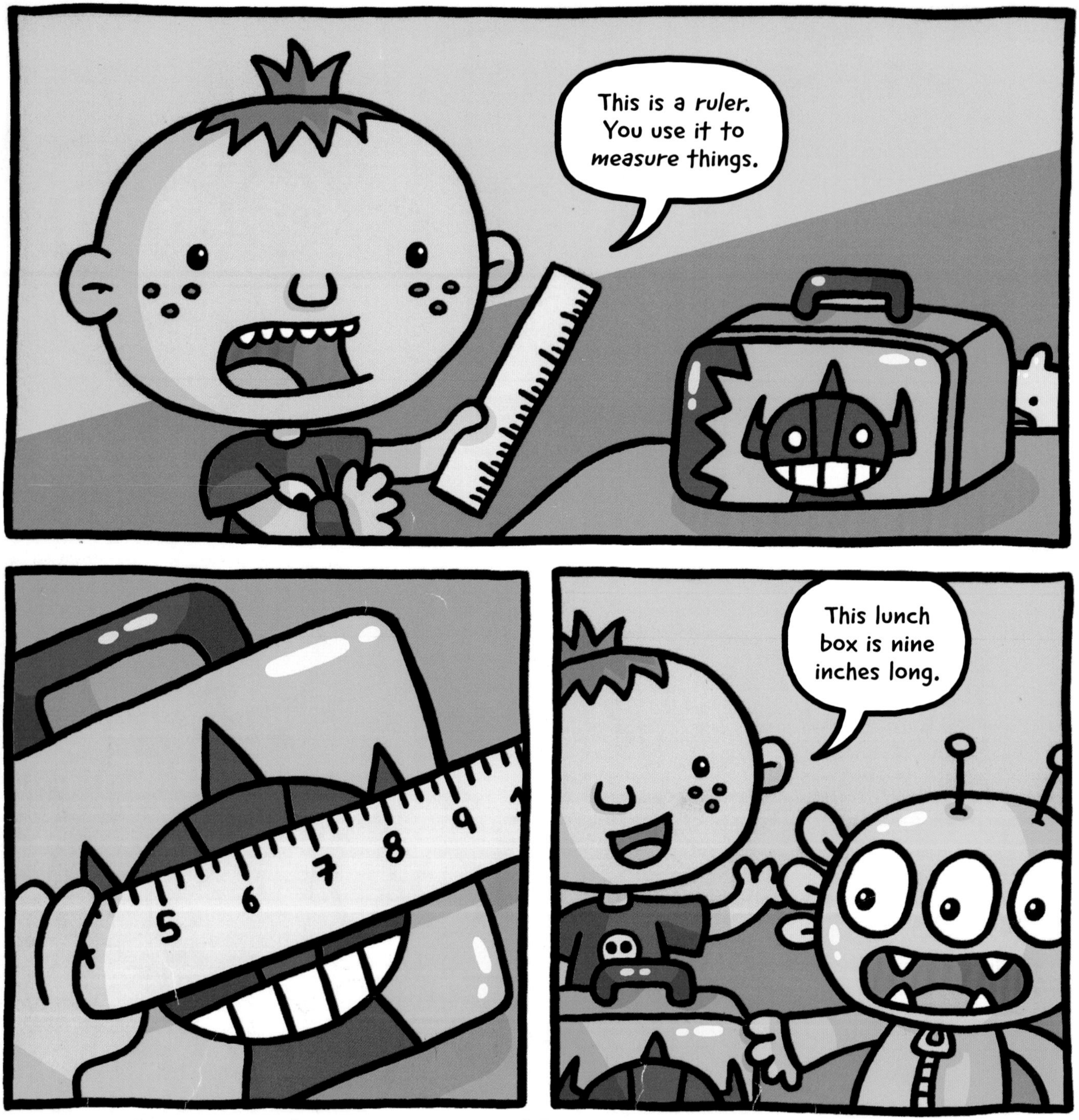
This is a *ruler*. You use it to *measure* things.
This lunch box is nine inches long.

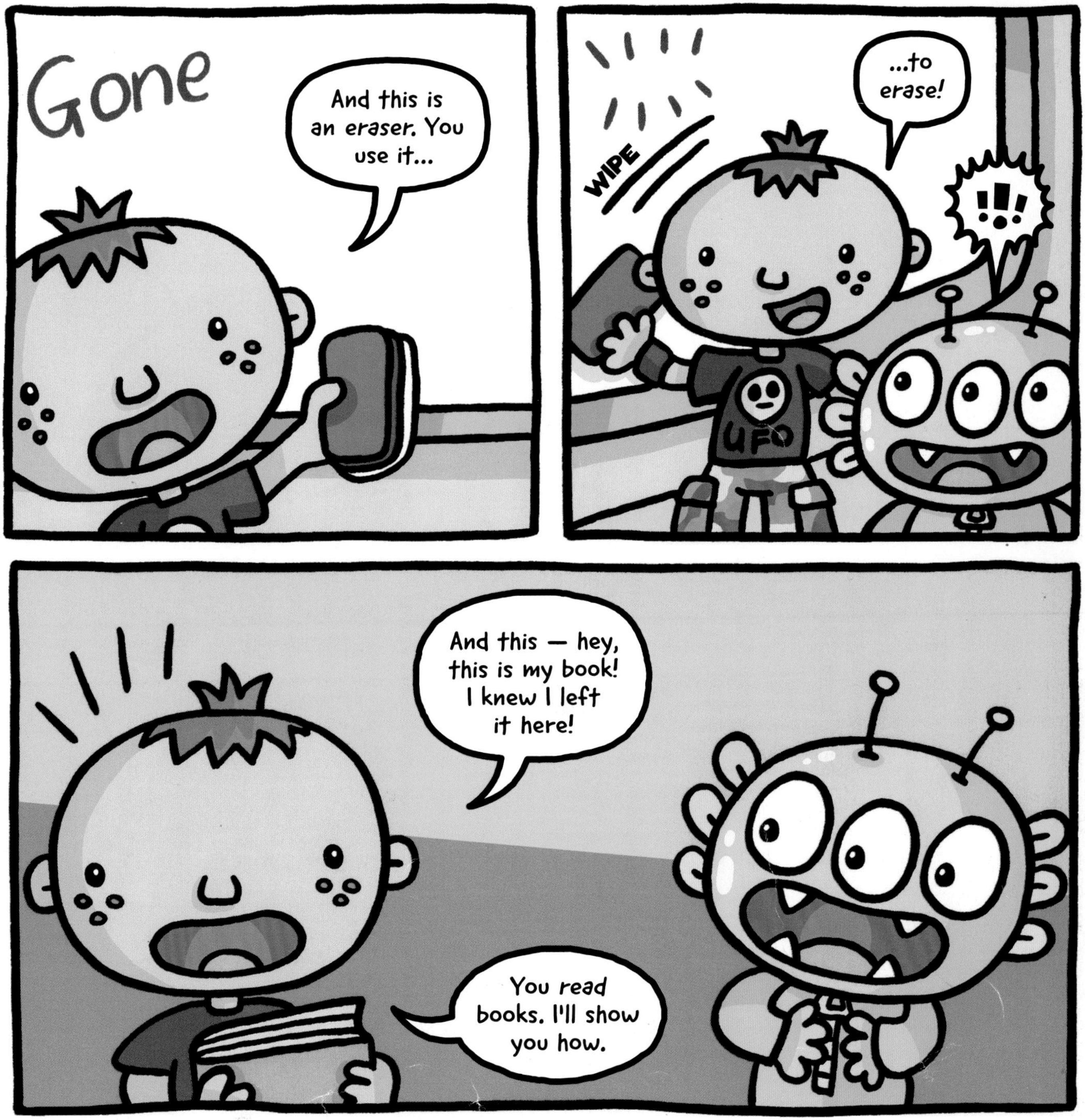
Gone
And this is an eraser. You use it...
WIPE
...to erase!
!!!
And this — hey, this is my book! I knew I left it here!
You read books. I'll show you how.

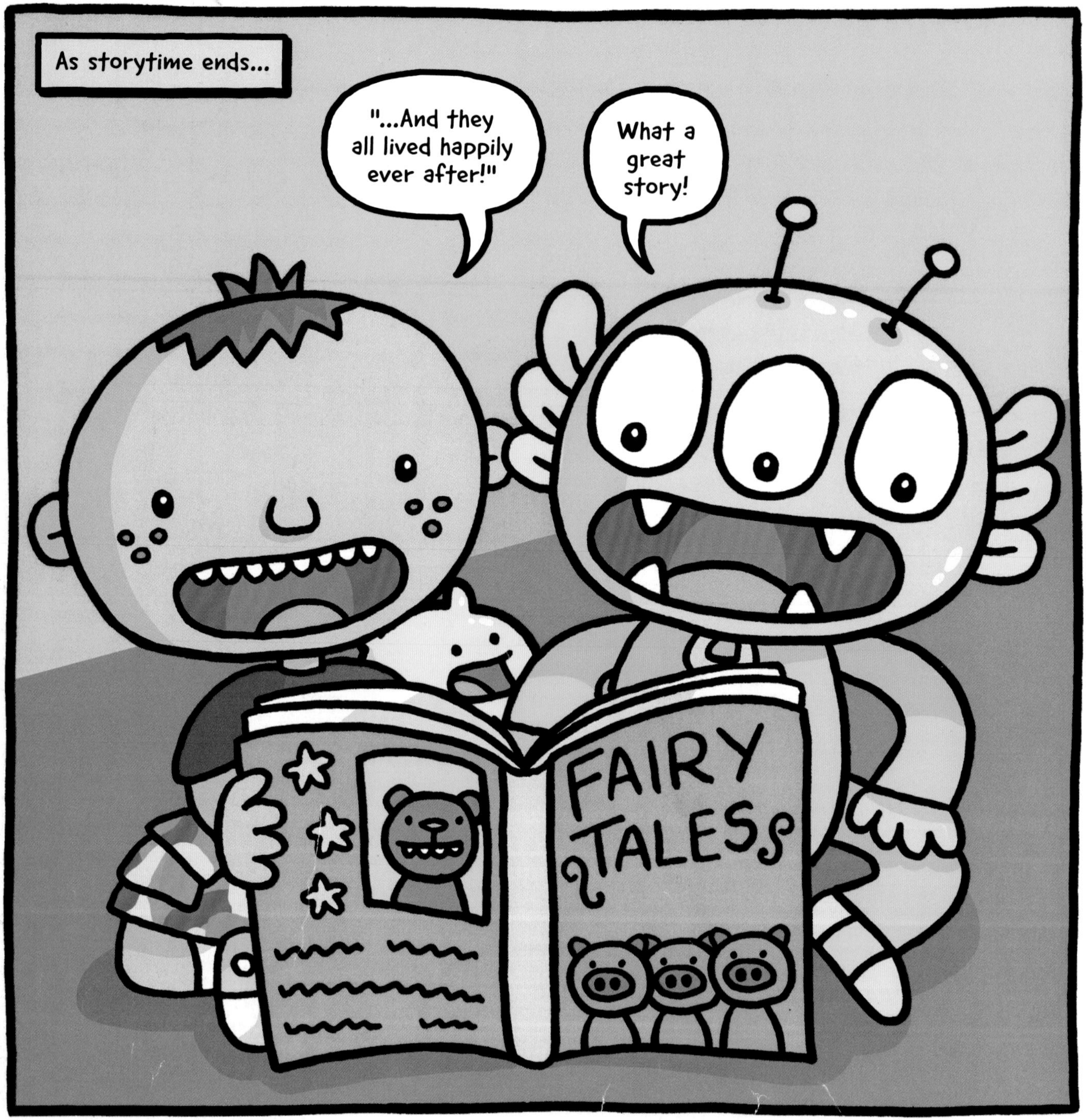
As storytime ends...
"...And they all lived happily ever after!"
What a great story!
FAIRY TALES

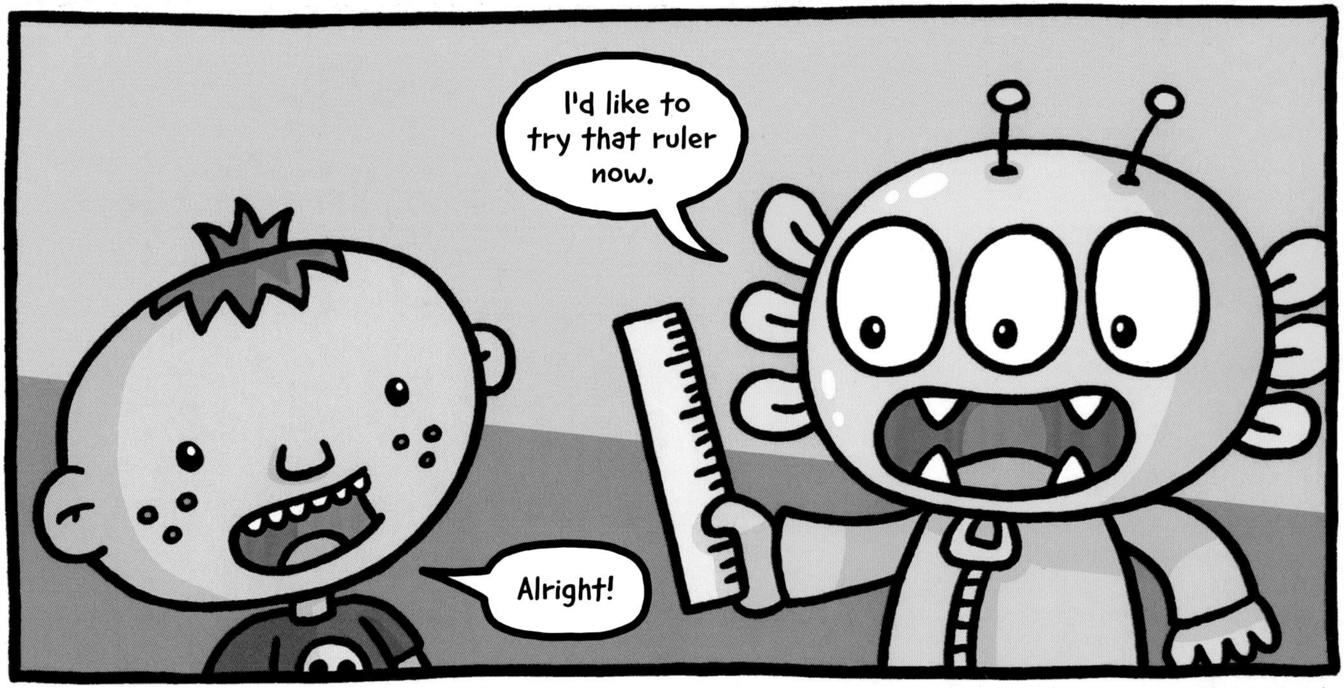
I'd like to try that ruler now.
Alright!

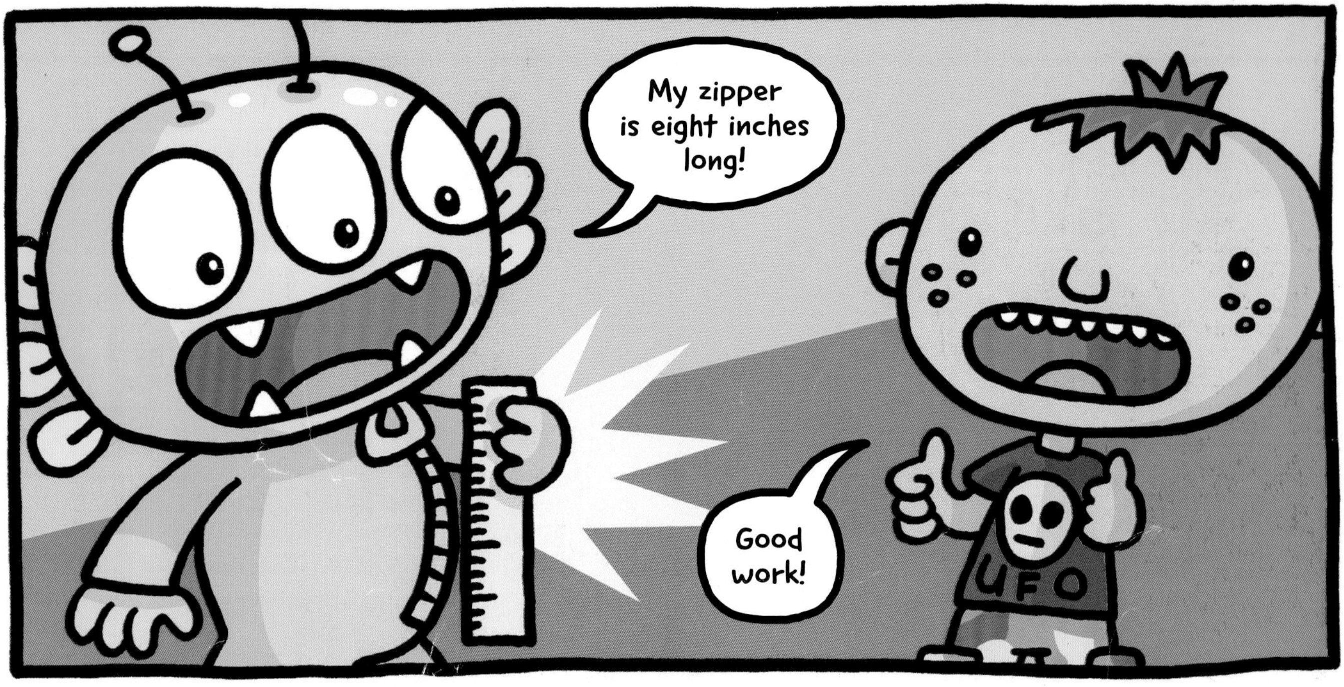
My zipper is eight inches long!
Good work!
UFO

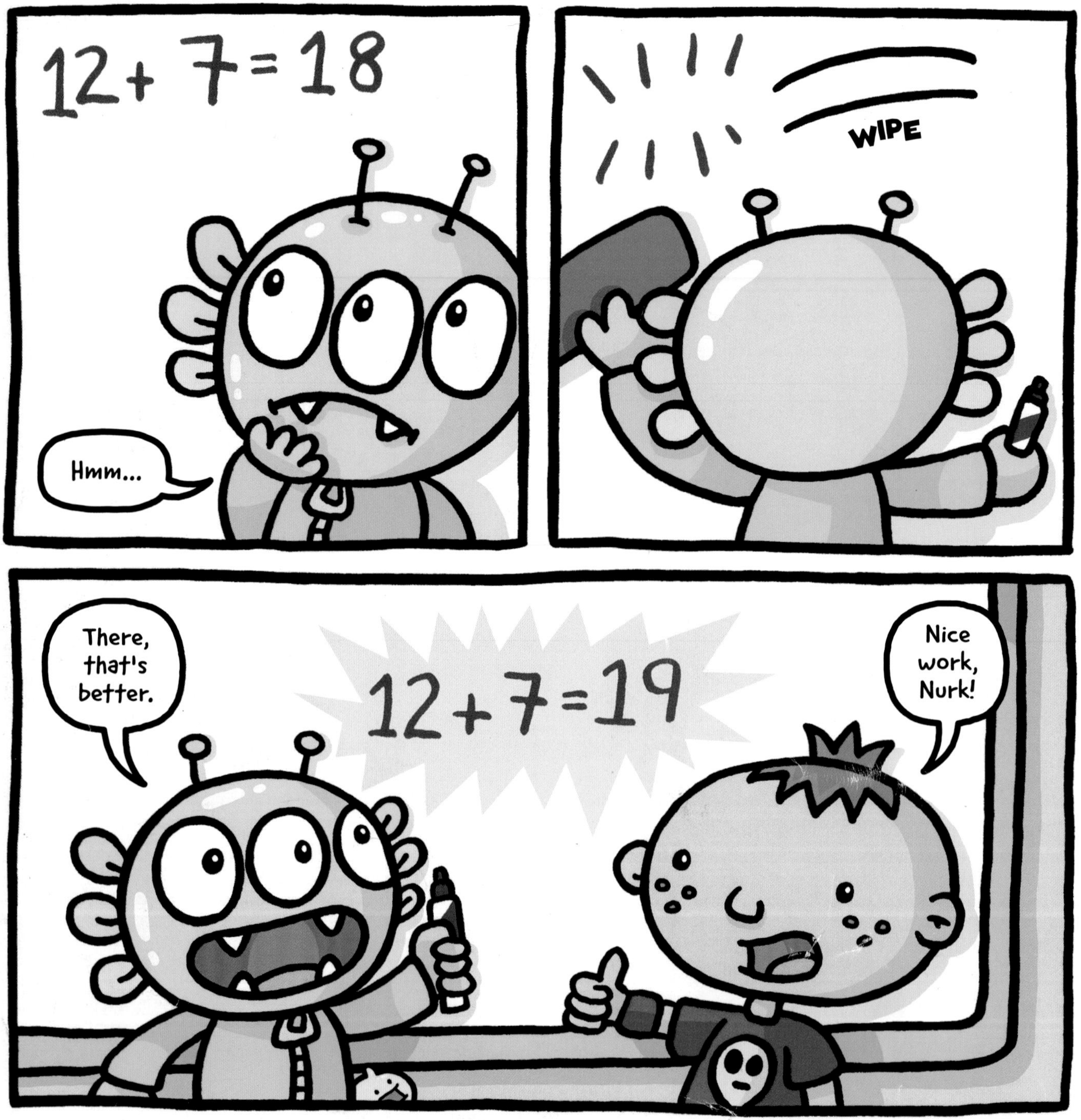
12 + 7 = 18
Hmm...
WIPE
There, that's better.
12 + 7 = 19
Nice work, Nurk!

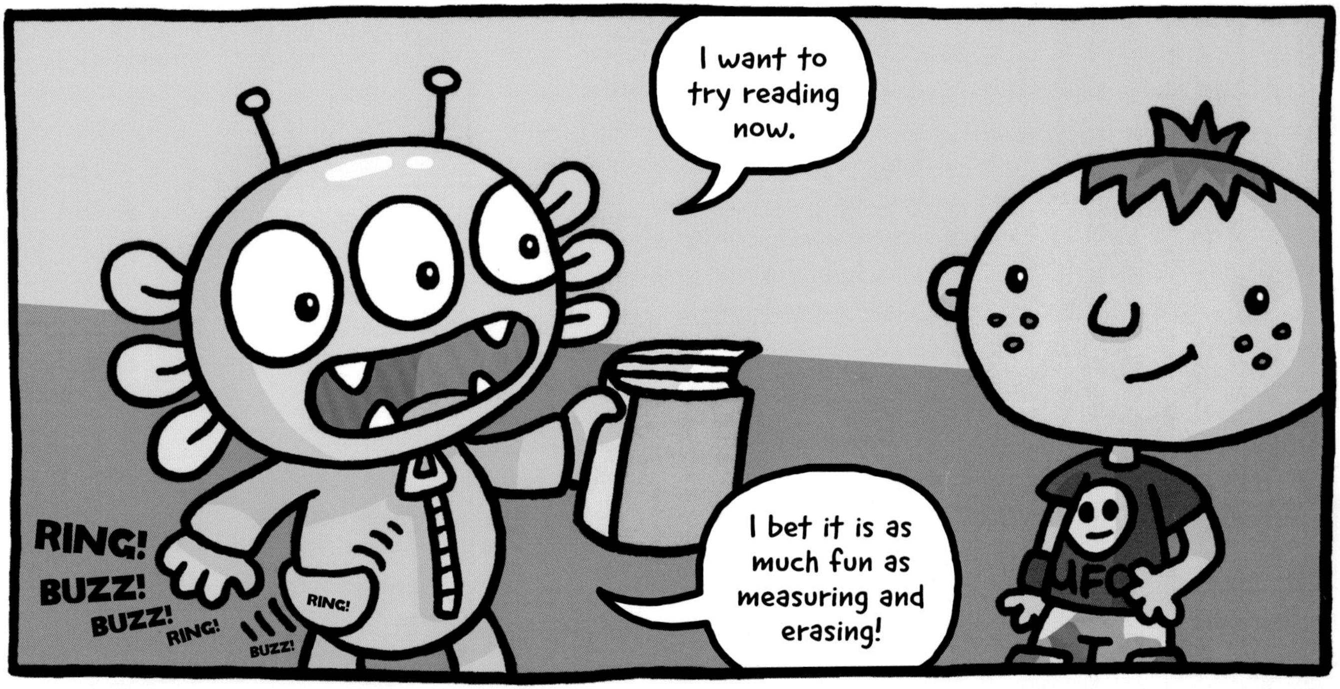
I want to try reading now.
I bet it is as much fun as measuring and erasing!
RING!
BUZZ!
BUZZ!
RING!
RING!
BUZZ!
UFO

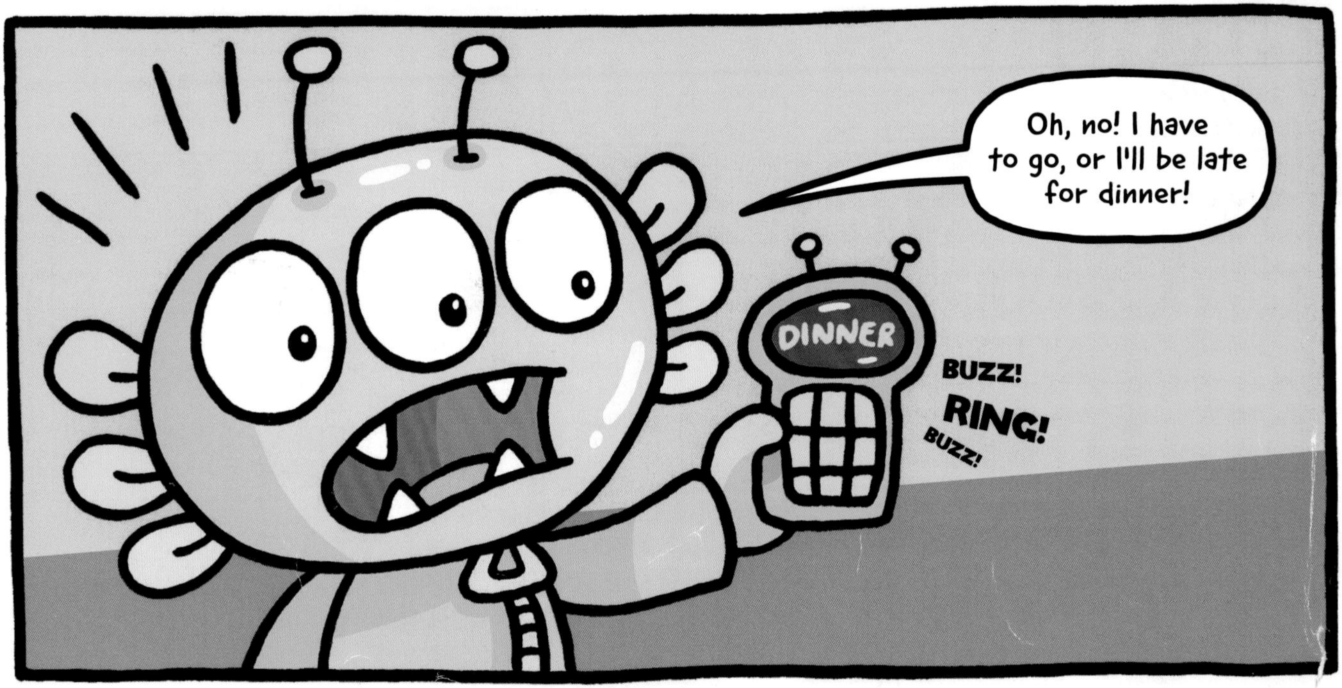
Oh, no! I have to go, or I'll be late for dinner!
DINNER
BUZZ!
RING!
BUZZ!

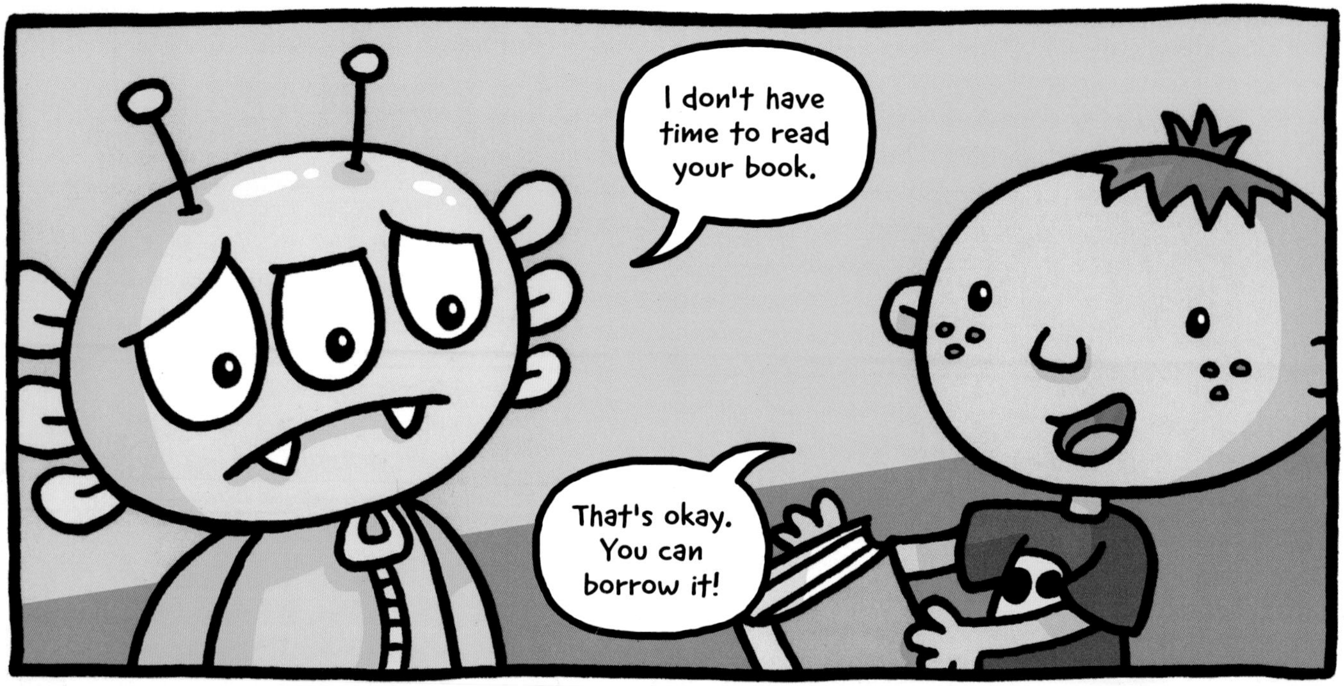
I don't have time to read your book.
That's okay. You can borrow it!

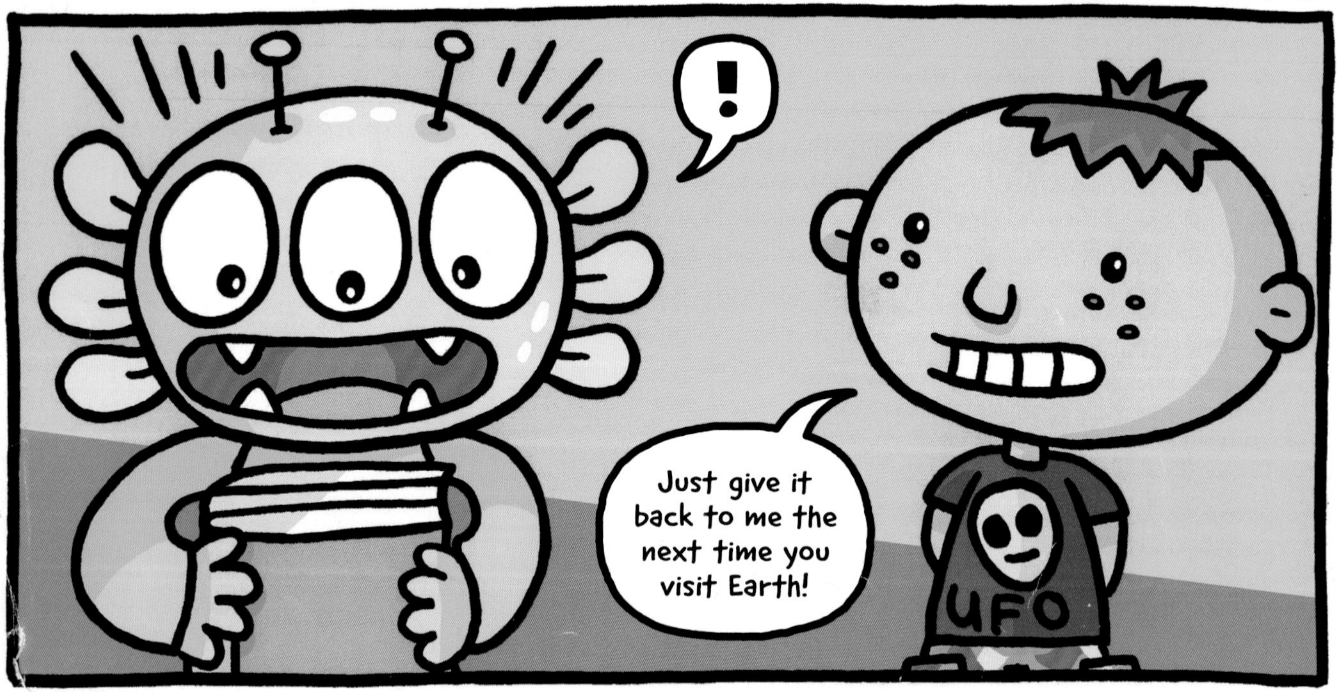
!
Just give it back to me the next time you visit Earth!
UFO

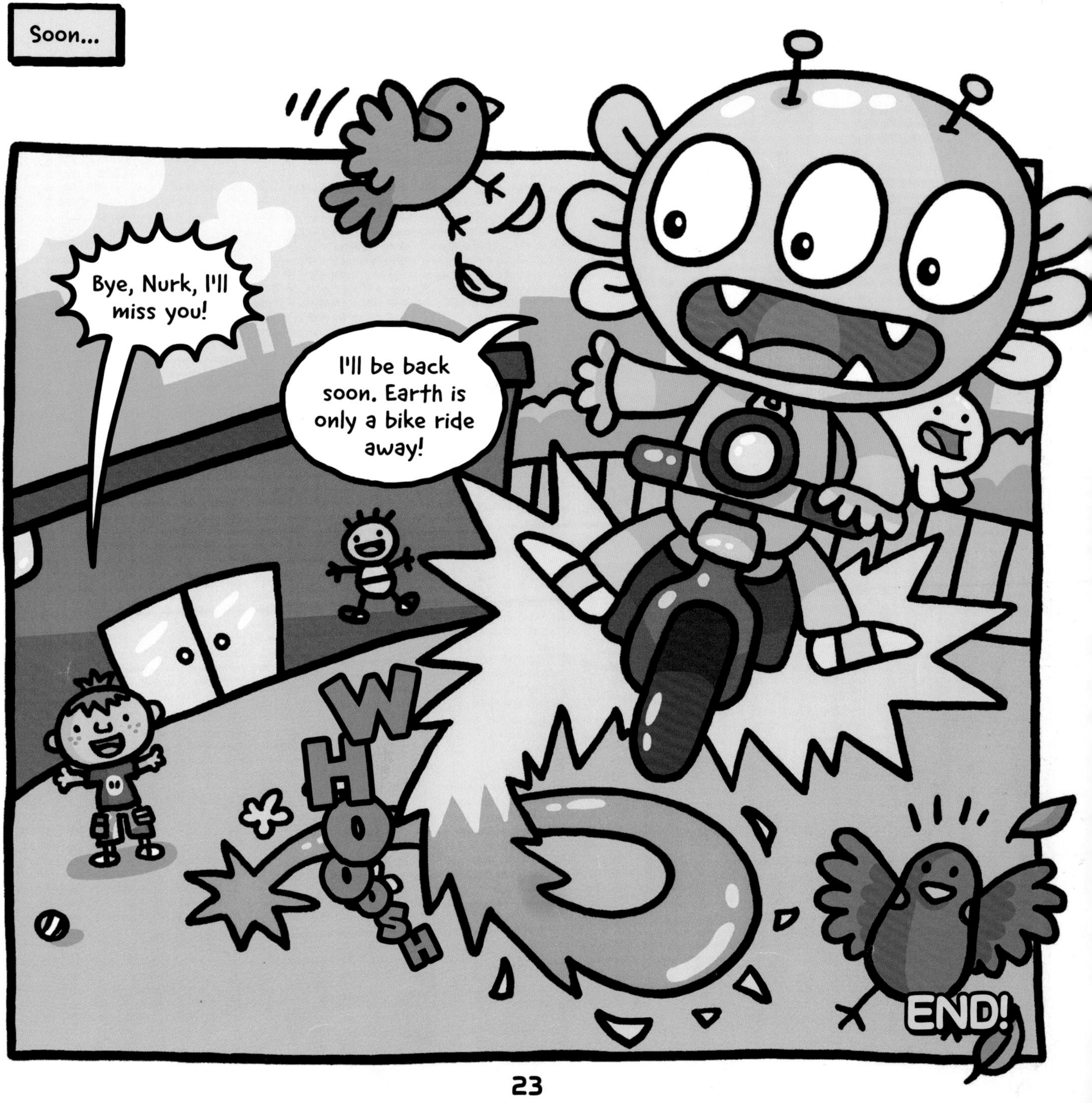
Soon...
Bye, Nurk, I'll miss you!
I'll be back soon. Earth is only a bike ride away!
WHOOSH
END!

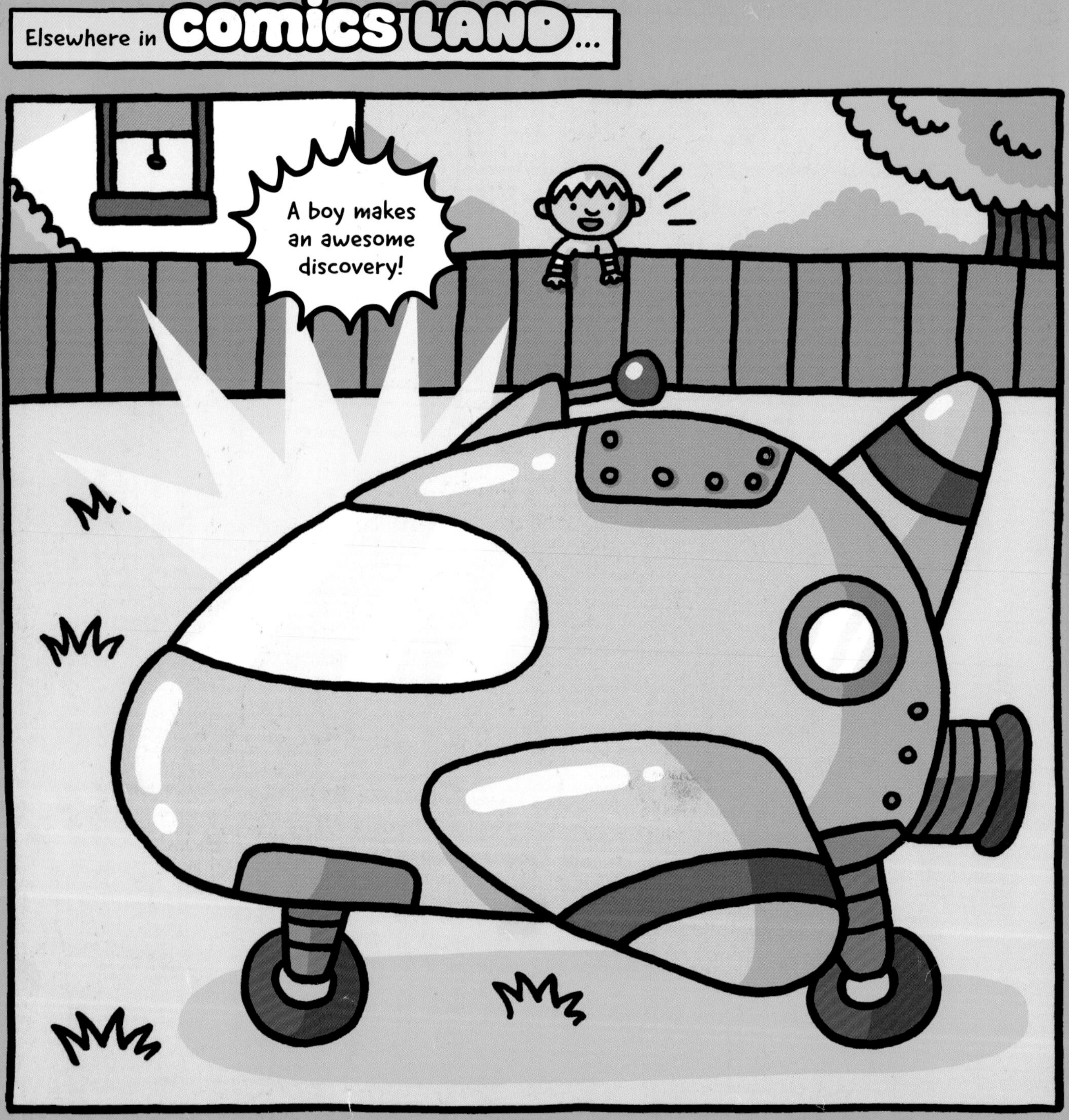
Elsewhere in COMICS LAND...
A boy makes an awesome discovery!

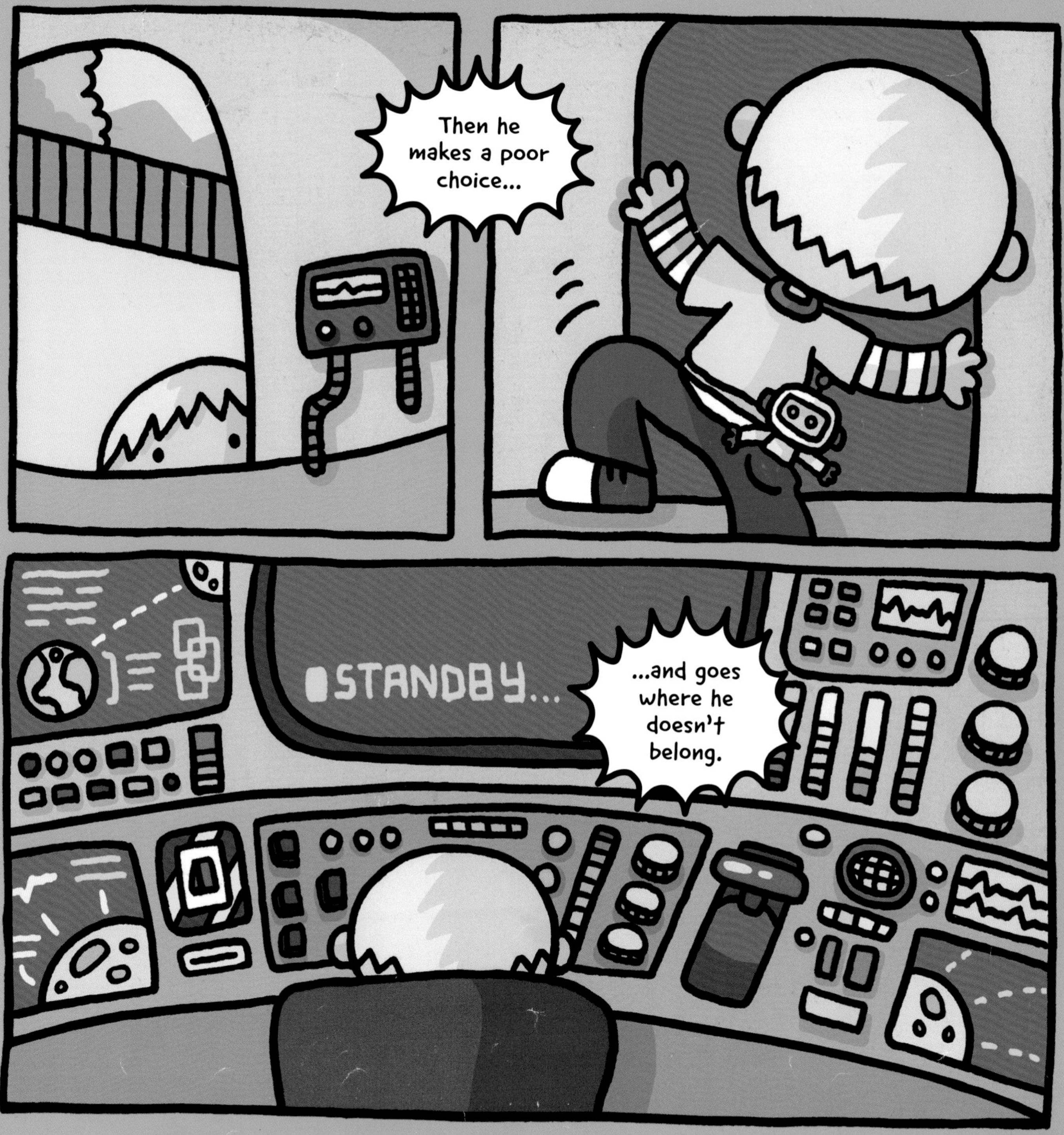
Then he makes a poor choice...
STANDBY...
...and goes where he doesn't belong.

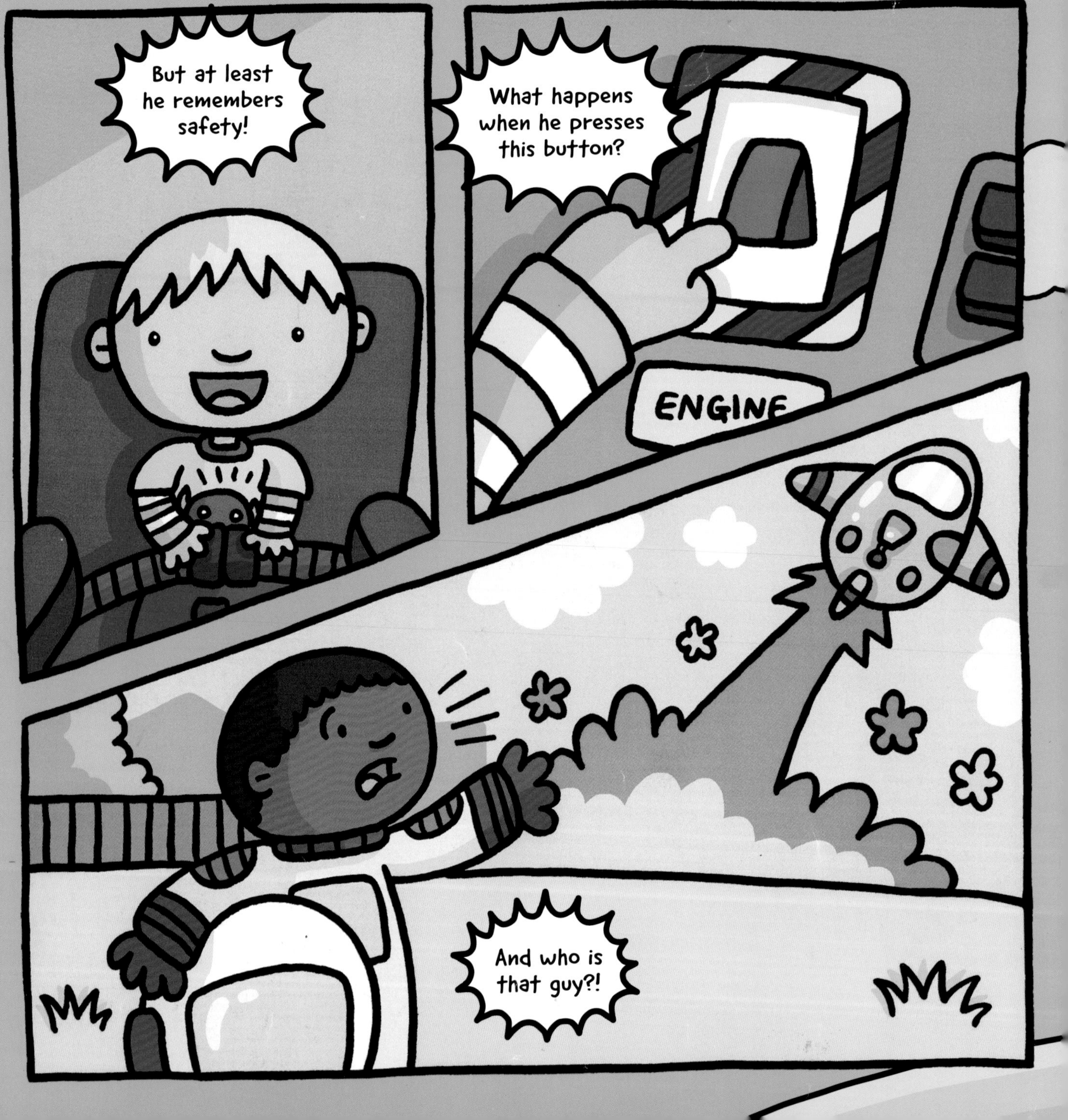
But at least he remembers safety!
What happens when he presses this button?
ENGINE
And who is that guy?!

Find out in the pages of...

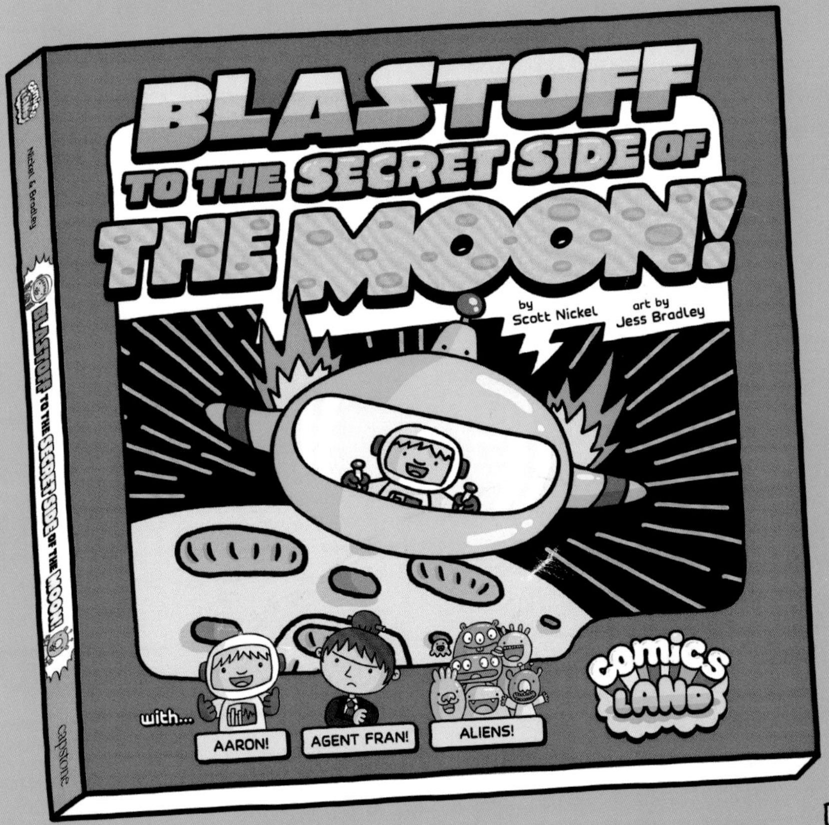
BLASTOFF TO THE SECRET SIDE OF THE MOON!
by Scott Nickel
art by Jess Bradley
with...
AARON!
AGENT FRAN!
ALIENS!
COMICS LAND
Nickel & Bradley
capstone

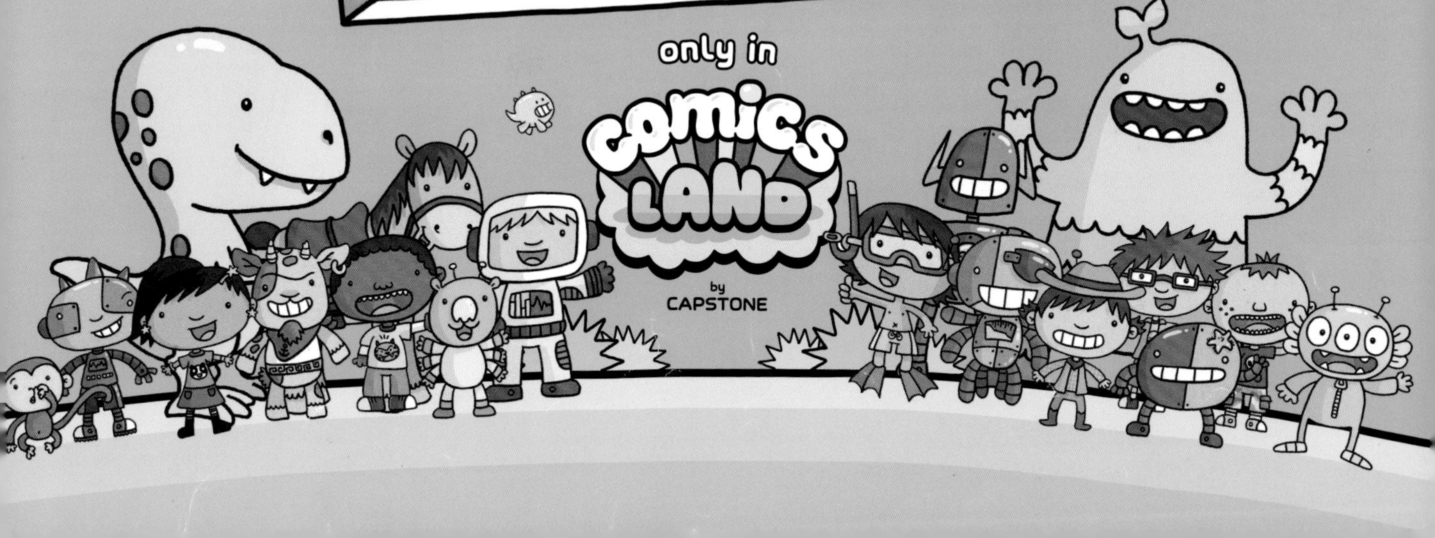
only in
COMICS LAND
by CAPSTONE

The New Kid from Planet Glorf

PRESENTS

GAME TIME!

Every box, balloon, and burst in a comic has a special name and job. Can you match the object with its name?

A. SOUND BURST

B. SURPRISE LINES

C. EXCITEMENT BALLOON

D. WORD BALLOON

E. MOTION LINES

F. SOUND EFFECT

G. NARRATIVE BOX

H. THOUGHT BALLOON

1
2
3
4
5
6
7
8
POW!
!

1=D, 2=H, 3=G, 4=A, 5=E, 6=B, 7=F, 8=C

Unscramble the letters to reveal words from the story.

1. ELANI	5. LURRE
2. NLAASDS	6. OBKO
3. XGAYLA	7. FLRGO
4. NELTPA	8. OHLSOC

1. ALIEN, 2. SANDALS, 3. GALAXY, 4. PLANET, 5. RULER, 6. BOOK, 7. GLORF, 8. SCHOOL

FIND THE PUPPY!

Go back and take another look at the story. You might notice that Nurk's puppy pops up everywhere, including Earth! Try to find him 10 times.

THE NEW KID FROM PLANET GLORF

PRESENTS

DRAW COMICS!

Want to make your own comic about Nurk? Start by learning to draw the little alien. Comics Land artist Jess Bradley shows you how in six easy steps!

You will need:

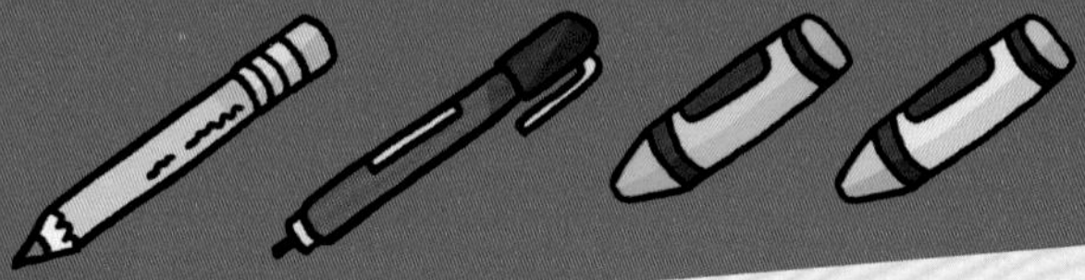

1.

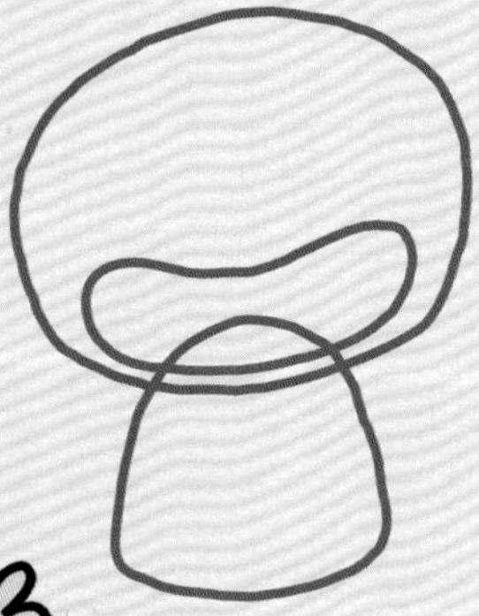

2.

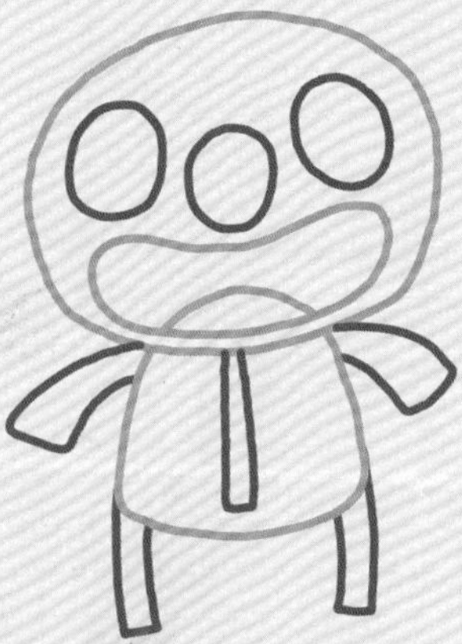

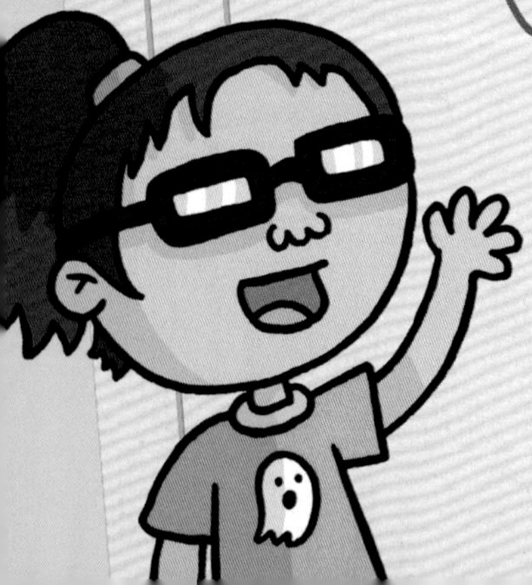

Draw with pencil!

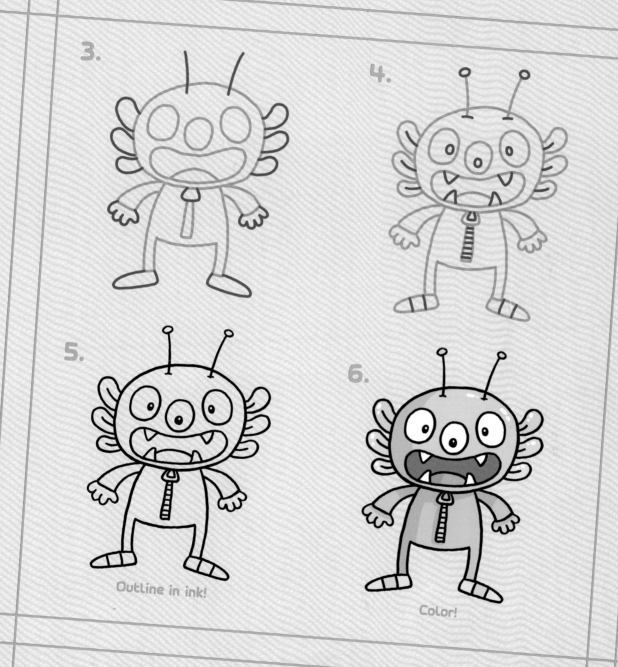

3.

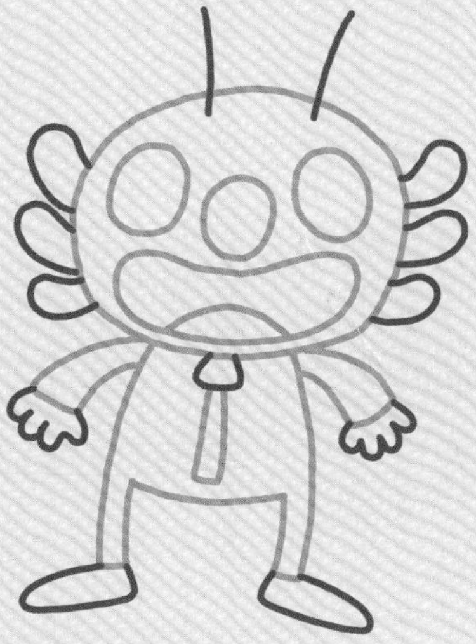

4.

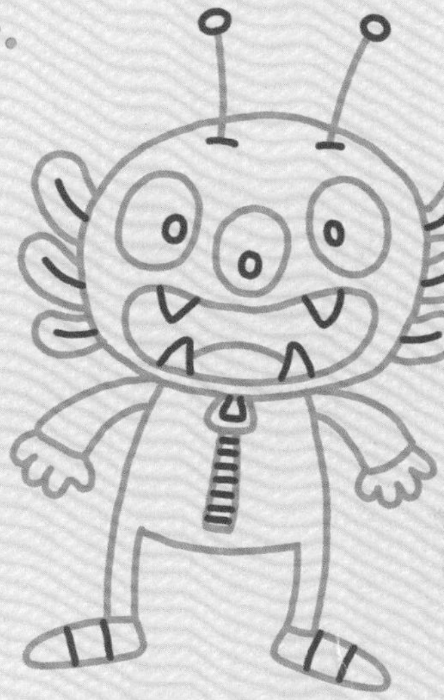

5.

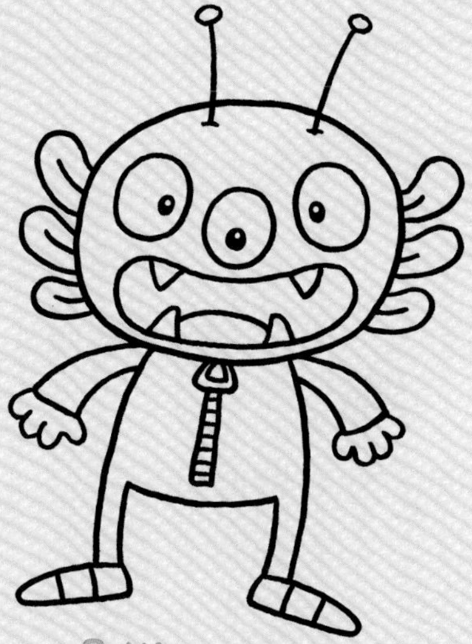

Outline in ink!

6.

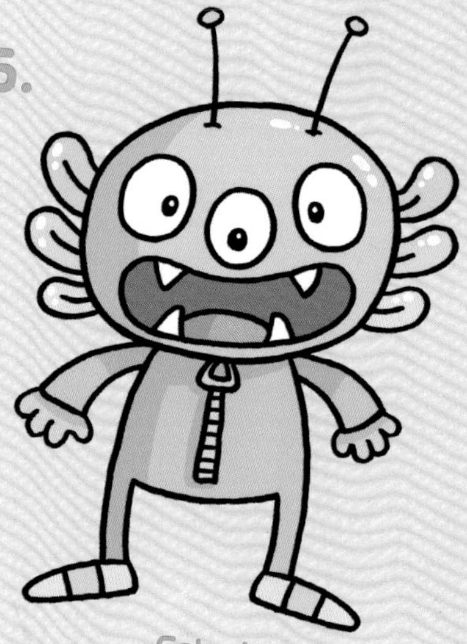

Color!

ARIE KAPLAN

WRITER

As a comic book writer, Arie Kaplan has written stories for DC Comics, Archie Comics, Bongo Comics, IDW, Papercutz, *MAD Magazine*, *Nickelodeon Magazine*, and Grosset & Dunlap. Arie is also a nonfiction author and video game writer.

JESS BRADLEY

ARTIST

Jess Bradley is an illustrator living and working in Bristol, England. She likes playing video games, painting, and watching bad films. Jess can also be heard to make a high-pitched "squeeeee" when excited, usually while watching videos clips of otters or getting new comics in the mail.

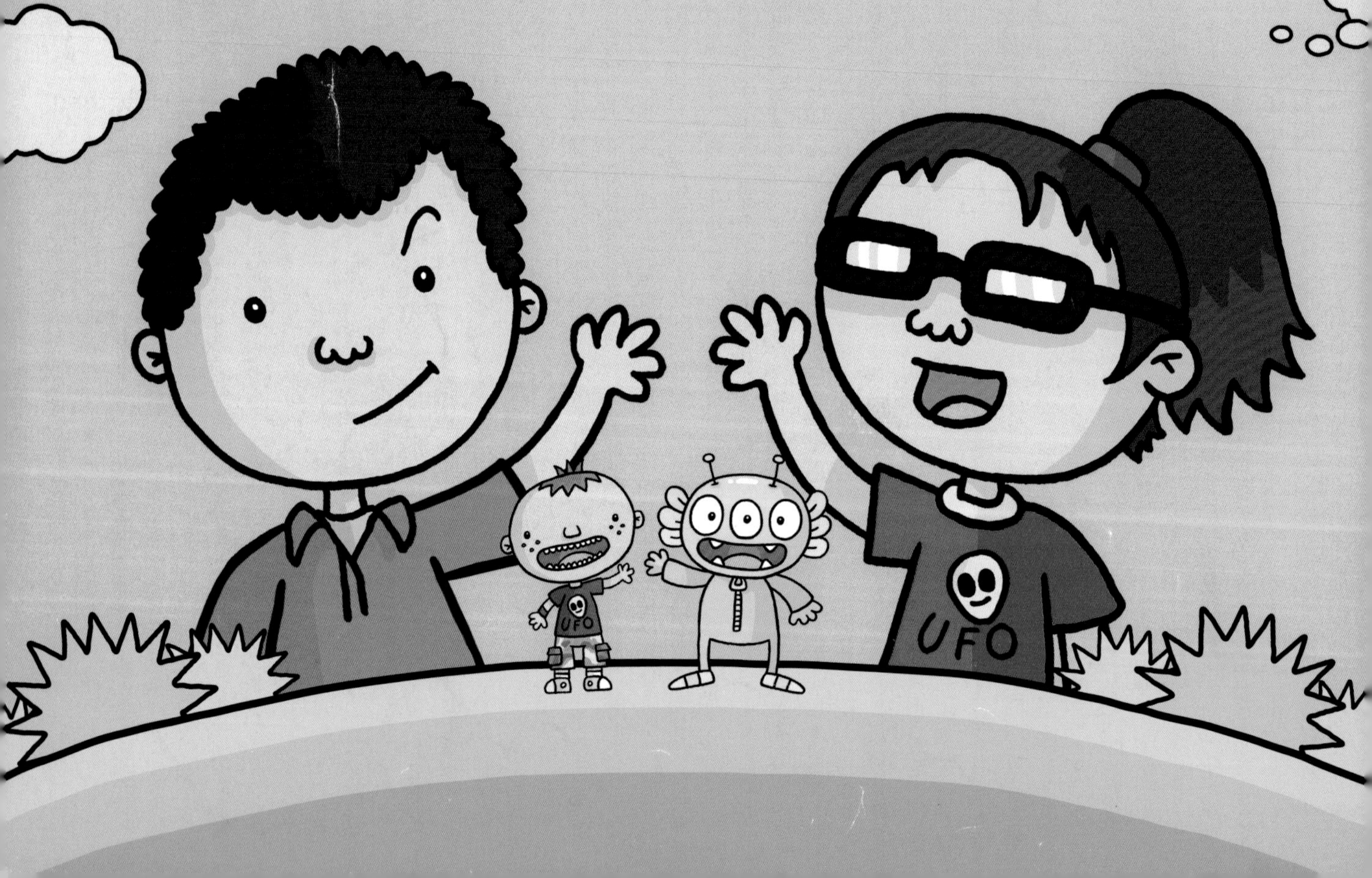
UFO
UFO